AMERICA'S FAVORITE CHRISTMASTOWN

Dawn Klinge

Also by Dawn Klinge

Sorrento Girl

Palmer Girl

Biltmore Girl

Dawn Klinge
www.dawnklinge.com

Publisher's Note: This is a work of fiction. Names, characters, places, and incidents are a product of the author's imagination. Locales and public names are sometimes used for atmospheric purposes. Any resemblance to actual people, living or dead, or to businesses, companies, events, institutions, or locales is completely coincidental.

Book Layout ©2017 BookDesignTemplates.com

America's Favorite Christmastown/ Dawn Klinge. -- 1st ed.
ISBN 978-1-7346434-3-5

To Darcie Graves, my sister and friend

Snow was falling,
so much like stars
filling the dark trees
that one could easily imagine
its reason for being was nothing more
than prettiness.

—Mary Oliver

CHAPTER ONE

"Hold on, babe. Do I have lipstick on my teeth?" Alexis Jacobson finished adjusting her camera, then flashed a monkey grin. It usually gained a laugh, but not this time.

"No, you're fine. Let's get this done." Nick Andrews reached for his prop—a mug of hot cocoa topped with an artfully swirled dollop of whipped cream. Alexis hit record and hurried toward her place on the sofa. The edge in Nick's voice didn't escape her notice, but Alexis brushed it off.

They'd pulled the sofa close to the large stone fireplace; its warm, glowing logs crackled softly, contributing to the scene's cozy ambiance. Also within the camera's frame of view was a majestic Christmas tree, which featured sparkly white lights, silver mercury globes, and a thick, red-velvet ribbon woven throughout the branches. Alexis curled her wool-sock-clad feet underneath her body and cuddled close to Nick, who wrapped his free arm around her and pulled her toward him. She breathed in the scent of bug spray and sunblock. Otherwise, the Christmas vibe was perfect for the filming of the Woods Resort holiday campaign.

Everything on camera was carefully curated: low lighting, candlelight, festive music, a plate of gingerbread cookies on the coffee table, and a happy couple. Nick and Alexis appeared to have come in from a day on the slopes with their coordinating Nordic sweaters. They were professionals, and they made a great team. They knew what their viewers wanted.

Alexis waited for a few beats, took a sip of cocoa from her mug, then smiled sweetly at Nick as he leaned over and gently kissed the top of her head. He played his part well. Then Alexis pulled away. "Okay, I think we got it!" She jumped off the couch and lunged toward the camera to stop the recording.

Nick's phone pinged as he stood. Nick's phone pinged as he stood up to pull off his sweater. Grabbing his phone, he read the newest message and mumbled, "Good," before turning to Alexis. "Okay, if we're done here, I'm going down to the bar to work before dinner."

Alexis waved as he bounded past her and opened the cabin's front door, allowing hot summer air and sunlight to pour in. Before the door closed, she caught a glimpse of the mountain resort's pool in the distance, where the excited shrieks of kids playing and splashing in the water offered a strange contrast to Nat King Cole singing about chestnuts roasting on an open fire through the Bluetooth speaker behind her. The pool beckoned invitingly. It would be cool and refreshing, but that would have to wait. They weren't on vacation. They were here to work, and she still needed to finish editing their latest YouTube video before it posted the next day.

Releasing a sigh, Alexis pulled back the curtains and watched Nick walk away.

Did Nick feel the same way she did? Stifled? How long could they go on like this? Alexis brushed away the loneliness that crept around the edges of her mind as she changed into a pair of jean shorts and a tank top before twisting her long, dark hair into a messy bun on the top of her head. She returned to the main room to switch off the fireplace and turn the music to a pop station. Christmas in July was over.

The next morning, she and Nick would board a six o'clock flight out of Denver to Puerto Vallarta, where they had been invited to spend the next three days recording videos for a new resort., The goal was to showcase its white sandy beaches, luxury rooms, and adventure tours before moving on to a five-star hotel in Banff, Canada. The travel never stopped.

Alexis had let go of the lease on her L.A. apartment more than two years ago, storing the few belongings she owned at her grandmother's house in Icicle Creek, Washington. What had started as a casual YouTube channel where she and Nick shared their travels had grown into a full-time business. Gone were the days of scraping together every penny they could save for their next adventure. Now resorts and hotels paid them to visit as their YouTube channel, Nick and Alexis, was closing in on three million subscribers. Many would consider it a dream job.

On camera, they tasted new foods, joked around, and brought viewers along as they explored the world together. They appeared to be a perfect, happy-go-lucky couple, but their brand was aspirational—a fantasy. They knew what their fans wanted, and they gave it to them. She was proud of what she and Nick had accomplished together. It wasn't easy, though. They often worked sixteen-hour days between filming, editing, and keeping up with their business.

Another hitch was their romance was no longer real. That had faded a long time ago. However, they remained friends, and their partnership worked, so they kept the illusion going. They had contracts to fulfill and expectations to meet. There was too much to lose if the truth got out.

Alexis donned her reading glasses on and opened her laptop. She only had two hours to finish editing their last video from Hawaii before meeting Nick for dinner in the restaurant at the main lodge. They'd go over next week's plans and divvy out the tasks. It was time to get to work.

***

The front door opened, and Nick called out, "You ready for dinner?"

Alexis was just putting the finishing touches on a video description she'd been writing. She stood and took a step away from the desk. Pins and needles pricked her right foot as she put weight on it, the result of sitting too long in one position. It was easy to lose track of time while she edited. "Yep. But first, do you want to take a look at this video before tomorrow?"

"Nah, I'm sure it's fine." Once again, there was an edge to Nick's voice. He seemed distracted; was something bothering him?

Alexis grabbed her purse, ensuring she had her phone and turned off the lamp before following Nick out the door.

Once in the restaurant, they sat in a dark booth towards the back of the room. The atmosphere was old school, upscale, and romantic. Alexis perused the menu. Lamb chops or chicken parmesan?

Nick put down his menu and looked at her He hesitated, bringing weight to the words that followed. "We need to talk."

CHAPTER TWO

Alexis lingered over the cup of hot tea she'd ordered after her meal. She wanted to give Nick enough time to pack his things and leave before she headed back up the hill toward the cabin. He'd booked a red-eye out of Denver, and a car would be picking him up soon.

It would be easier this way. Less messy. Goodbyes were never easy, even though this one had been a long time coming. Much to her surprise, she felt more relief than anger—or sadness. But tension and uncertainty gnawed in the back of her mind.

The conversation had been calm and businesslike. It was a logical next step that Alexis had been half-expecting—though some advance notice would have been appreciated. His words swirled through her thoughts. "I can't do this anymore—this pretending. I got a job offer in Seattle, and I took it. I'm leaving right away. I'm sorry."

Like Nick, Alexis was also tired of keeping up the pretense. Unfortunately for her, she didn't have any other employment lined up. What now? What would they tell their subscribers?

And their sponsors? Without Nick, she didn't have a YouTube channel. They'd been a package deal.

She inhaled the delicate citrus scent of the tea wafting up from the porcelain cup in her hands. The dreamy notes of a melancholy song coming from a piano in the corner of the room provided the perfect soundtrack to her current mood. Tears threatened to spill from the corners of her eyes, but she blinked them back. This is what she'd wanted—a fresh start. Freedom. New opportunities. Right? Alexis would not have guessed that Nick would be the one to call it off first. That reality stung a little.

"Is there anything else I can get for you, Miss?" The server asked. "More hot water for your tea?"

"No—no, thank you. Just the check, please."

"Your friend already took care of it."

"Oh? Okay." Considering the predicament he'd left her in, it was the least he could do.

***

Back at the cabin, Alexis stared at the clock on the wall, mentally calculating the time in Washington state. Was it too late to call Oma? Plopping down on the couch, Alexis pulled a blanket over her legs and made the call. She waited only a moment before Oma's sweet voice answered, "Hello, dear."

"Oma—I just wanted to say hello. How's everything at home?"

"Well, I have some news for you!" Oma sang. "I'm getting into the vacation rental business. Remember that old Lake Haven Retreat Center you went to when you were thirteen? I bought it! Or, it will be mine soon, after the paperwork is done. Of course, there's some repair work to do first, but I can handle it."

Alexis was only slightly surprised by Oma's announcement. Several years ago, on their way to get a Christmas tree, Oma had taken her by the place. A little work was an understatement.

Lake Haven Retreat had once been a charming sleepaway camp with rustic cabins, canoes, and a grand lodge nestled in the woods. It was a few miles up the mountain from town, on the shores of Snow Lake. Years ago, the owners put the camp up for sale, but when there were no takers, they simply moved away, leaving the property to fall into disrepair.

Nevertheless, Oma's eyes sparkled like a child's whenever she brought up her idea of buying the place and turning it into short-term vacation rentals. Yet Oma was getting along in years and wasn't a wealthy woman. How could she afford it?

"Oma, are you sure you want to start a new business right now?" Alexis asked. "That sounds like an awful lot of work to do on your own. You deserve to relax on a beach. Why would you want to be burdened with a new business?"

"Ah, honey, it's just a few broken windows— nothing paint and some fresh flowers won't fix. You know me, dear. I need my projects. And this is something I've wanted to do for a long time." Oma paused a moment. "I know, come and visit! Maybe you and Nick could make one of your videos for Lake Haven? My goal is to have the cabins available for rent before Christmas."

"Yeah... uh, about that. I have something to tell you, too." Alexis sighed. She knew Oma loved Nick, which is why she had never confessed that their relationship was over. "Nick and I have decided to go our separate ways."

The ensuing silence was long enough that Alexis wondered if her phone had disconnected. Then Oma's gentle voice responded, "I'm sorry, honey. How do you feel about that?"

"I'm not sure. This also means I don't have a job anymore." Alexis's voice cracked with emotion. "What am I going to do?"

"You'll figure it out, dear. You always do. But for now, why don't you come home?"

Home. The word made her heart feel a little twinge of regret. How long had it been since she'd been there? Two years? Her job had taken her around the world and brought many exciting opportunities, but they hadn't come without sacrifices. She'd been too busy to visit.

Since the age of twelve, when Alexis lost her parents, Oma had been her safe harbor. Icicle Creek had become her home. She hadn't always shown her grandmother the gratitude she felt in return. In fact, as a teen dealing with the pain of her loss, Alexis knew she'd been downright obnoxious at times.

"Remember, home is a shelter from all sorts of storms," her grandmother continued, bringing Alexis back to the present.

Oma always knew what to say. It felt as though a storm was closing in—an awful one. Alexis sighed as she considered the overwhelming list of things she now needed to do. The resort in Puerto Vallarta would be the first company she'd need to reach out to and offer an apology. Would there be consequences for backing out of the contracts? Probably. That mess, however, could be cleaned up anywhere she had Wi-Fi.

Oma needed her—and Alexis needed Oma. Maybe going home would allow her an opportunity to talk some sense into her grandmother before she made a huge mistake and bought that money pit of a camp. Hopefully, it wasn't too late.

Alexis sank back against the pillows on the couch and sighed. "Thank you, Oma. I think I'll do that. I'm coming home."

***

Lightning flashed across the dark sky seconds before the plane lurched. Alexis reached to steady the cup of coffee on the tray table, but it was too late. It tipped, spilling onto her lap. While she dabbed at the mess with a napkin, the captain's voice came over the speaker.

"Folks, please return to your seats. I've turned on the seatbelt sign. Unfortunately, we've hit a little bit of turbulence, which is going to delay our arrival in Seattle. We apologize for the inconvenience."

Alexis felt her heart sink at the announcement. How much of a delay were they talking about? She had a connecting flight to catch and not much wiggle room with her layover to account for a delay. As far as she knew, there was still only one flight per day going into Pangborn airport.

Taking a deep breath, Alexis steeled herself with a fresh resolve to "go with the flow." That was her new motto—or at least she was trying to make it so. There was no point in getting worked up about what she couldn't control.

Two hours later, the plane touched down at SeaTac. It had been a chaotic ride, but they'd made it safely, albeit a half-hour too late. Alexis sighed as she glanced at the time on her phone —nine-fifteen. Could she get a rental car at this hour? It wasn't too far to drive, and it was preferable to sleeping in the airport or finding a hotel at the last minute. As soon as the pilot gave the all-clear to turn their devices on, she sent off a quick text to Oma, letting her know about the delay and telling her not to bother going to the local airport to pick her up.

Alexis walked into an airport bustling with far more people than she expected for that time of night. Outside the windows, rain slashed down in large sheets that bounced off the runway. Ahead of her, the word "canceled" repeated down the columns on the digital flight board. Quite a storm. Alexis picked up her pace as she headed toward the rental counter, knowing that if it were still open, she wouldn't be the only one trying to get a car tonight.

She was right. Alexis got in line behind at least twenty other people vying for a car from the only rental agency still open. I might get lucky, she thought optimistically. She looked down at the coffee stain on her white jeans. It looked terrible, but what could she do? Give up her place in line to slip away to change? Not a chance.

Alexis scrolled through Instagram as the line slowly inched forward until there was just one man ahead of her. Even though she couldn't see his face, he seemed vaguely familiar. Alexis studied him with interest, finally getting a better look at him when he turned to get something out of his bag. Recognition clicked. There stood her old high school crush—Justin Karon, still as handsome as ever.

This was unexpected. The rumor was that he'd moved to DC and worked at some high-powered political company. No surprise there. Everyone in their town knew Justin would succeed wherever he set his mind. From the look of his expensive suit, he'd done exactly that.

Justin, who still hadn't noticed her (not much had changed), proceeded to pay for his rental and stepped away from the counter. Embarrassed by her stained pants and unkempt appearance, Alexis decided to keep her head down and try to remain unseen as Justin walked past her.

She moved forward and offered a smile to the agent. The man shook his head and flipped a sign that said closed. "Sorry, Miss. I just rented out our last vehicle, and we're not expecting any more to come in until tomorrow."

"Wait! I'll take anything! Please, I need to get home." Alexis's entreaty went unheeded as the man walked away.

Grumbles moved through the line behind her as people realized their shared fate. What now? She found a chair and sat, letting out a big sigh.

"Alexis?"

Justin was standing in front of her, wearing a curious expression.

"Oh, Justin! Hey, what a surprise! What are you doing here?" Alexis felt her cheeks grow warm. Why did she feel so awkward? It wasn't high school anymore. She'd come a long way since then.

"I'm on my way home. What about you?"

"Oh? Home, to Icicle Creek? That's where I'm going, eventually."

"Yes, I live in Icicle Creek again, and I think I took the last car." Justin responded with a shrug. "Sorry about that. Do you want a ride? We're going to the same place; it wouldn't be any problem."

Alexis hesitated. How long had it been since they'd had a conversation? Ten years? And even then, she'd only ever known Justin from a distance. In high school, he'd been popular—student body president, star basketball player, Homecoming King. The cliche would have been a turn-off to Alexis if he hadn't also been so darn nice.

When she moved to Icicle Creek as a middle schooler, Justin had been one of the first people to introduce himself to her and offer a friendly smile. Throughout their school years, she'd had a thing for him—a secret she never shared with anyone. Back then, she'd been a shy, bookish girl who kept to herself. Other than a few occasions in English class their senior year, when they'd worked on group projects together, Alexis's path had rarely crossed his.

Justin was practically a stranger. Alexis was hardly in the mood to spend the next few hours making small talk in a car with someone she barely knew, no matter how charming he might be. Would she be crazy to say yes to his offer? Exhaustion blanketed her body. Her sleep-deprived eyes felt like they'd been rubbed with raw onion. Enough hesitating. She'd be crazy not to go with him. It was the fastest way to get home, and Justin was a good guy.

"Having some company will help me stay awake. You'd be doing me a favor." Justin smiled. His kind blue eyes sparkled, putting Alexis at ease.

"Well, then. Okay—thank you."

As Alexis grabbed her suitcase and followed her knight in shining armor toward the exit, the sound of a crying, overtired child punctuated the air. You and me both, kid. After the last twenty-four hours, she wanted nothing more than to be at home with Oma. Only a few more hours.

Justin found the car in the rental garage and let out a good-natured laugh. It was a tiny orange Fiat. "I hope all of our luggage will fit in this thing!"

The juxtaposition of Justin—at least six-and-a-half feet tall— in front of the miniature car made Alexis grin. "Are you sure you'll fit?" She teased.

A few minutes later, they had their answer. He fit—barely. Justin's knees practically bumped against his chin, but they were on the road. They'd successfully stuffed their suitcases in the back of the car. Alexis held a bag on her lap as there was no other option.

After Alexis finished texting Oma to let her know where she was, Justin pointed toward an exit sign off 1-90. "Are you hungry? There's a Taco Bell just ahead. We could go through the drive-through."

"Yes, I'm starving. I would love that."

Cute, caring, and considerate; was this guy too good to be true? Alexis's concern over not having the energy to make small talk for the next few hours evaporated as a realization dawned. She was actually enjoying Justin's company— especially after she had her tacos. The warm food in her belly was making her feel more at ease.

The rain continued to bucket down, making the road a shiny black mirror that reflected the oncoming headlights in blurry smudges. However, it didn't seem to bother Justin. His confidence behind the wheel helped Alexis relax.

What was Justin's story? She started with an easy question. "So, where were you flying in from tonight?"

"DC—I had some meetings out there the last few days. How about you?"

"Colorado."

Alexis didn't feel like elaborating. Maybe she'd chosen the wrong line of questioning. Perhaps Justin didn't want to explain what he'd been doing in DC any more than she wanted to tell him about why she'd been in Colorado. Did he know about her YouTube channel? After several years of being recognized frequently in public, she still felt awkward around people when it became apparent that they knew (or thought they knew) far more about her than she did about them.

Justin tried to get the conversation going again. "I've seen a couple of your YouTube videos. They're fantastic! It seems like you've been to some interesting places. Is that what you were doing in Colorado? Making a video?"

Darn, he knew.

"Ugh, yes—thank you. We were working on a Christmas campaign for a resort down there. How about you?" Alexis tried to bring the subject back to Justin. "What kind of business are you in?"

"Politics, real estate …." Justin gave a sheepish shrug. "I lived in DC for a while, up until about a couple of months ago when I moved back to Icicle Creek. And you? Where do you call home?"

"With the YouTube channel, I've been what some people might call a digital nomad for the last few years. But my grandmother still lives in Icicle Creek so I'll be staying with her while I'm there."

"Oh, wow. How long will you be in town?"

"I really don't know. A few weeks, maybe—"

"Well, I'm sure there will be many people who will be happy to see you. You're something of a celebrity in our little town." Justin fiddled with the buttons on the dash. "Mind if I turn on some music?"

Alexis felt her face grow warm. She brushed off his comment and attempted to turn the conversation another way. Music—focus on that. "Of course not. That would be good."

"Here." Justin handed his phone to Alexis. "Feel free to pick something you like from Spotify."

Alexis picked a Frank Sinatra playlist labeled as one of Justin's "favorites." She, too, loved the old standards. They spent the next couple of hours listening to music and chatting as the storm continued to rage outside. Justin was easy to talk to, and Alexis was happy about the events that led to their chance meeting. It felt as if hardly any time had passed when Justin pulled the orange Fiat up to the first stoplight in Icicle Creek.

Twinkly white lights adorned every building on Main Street. Even in the middle of summer, the Bavarian-themed village gave off a distinct Christmassy vibe. Alexis turned her gaze away from the view outside and checked the time on her phone—almost midnight. Would Oma still be awake? She started to give Justin directions to her grandmother's house.

"I know where Clarice's house is," Justin said. "We're old friends."

Old friends? This was news. Justin was full of surprises. "Oh?"

"Yeah, I've been helping her with a real estate deal."

"The camp?"

Justin turned the car onto the private road that led to Oma's. "Yeah. Exciting, right?"

Not exactly. Alexis took a deep breath in. So, Justin was behind this colossal mistake Oma was about to make? Not if she could help it.

CHAPTER THREE

The rich aroma of coffee wafted through the air. Alexis inhaled her favorite smell as she stretched her arms and adjusted her eyes to the morning light pouring through the sheer curtains of her old room. The rain had finally stopped, but not before the rhythmic sound of it tapping on the roof last night had sent her into the deepest sleep she'd had in a long while.

Alexis could hear Oma puttering around in the kitchen downstairs. The familiarity of the sounds and smells offered a soothing comfort. It was good to be home. She wanted to bask in the bliss of this fresh morning a few moments longer—before any talk of real estate, lost jobs, or broken relationships came up at breakfast.

After Justin dropped her off late last night, her grandmother greeted her with a warm hug and a promise to "talk in the morning." Oma wanted details. It was because she cared, Alexis knew, but that didn't make the idea of explaining her current situation any easier. The desire to please Oma and make her proud was always with Alexis. But right now, all she felt was shame over what she'd done. And then there was Oma's newest hair-brained idea to buy the camp. What was she going to do about that? Alexis hoped it wasn't too late to put a stop to it.

She got up, dressed, and made her way downstairs, where she joined Oma in the spacious farmhouse-style kitchen. "Good morning, Oma."

Oma turned and smiled. "Ah, good morning, sweetheart. You sleep well?"

"Yes, I did. Sorry I kept you up waiting so late last night."

"Dear, don't you worry about that. I'm glad you're here and that you made it home safely. How wonderful that you ran into Justin at Sea-Tac." Oma took Alexis's old rainbows-and-unicorn mug out of the cupboard and poured coffee into it. "That man, he's an angel. He's been advising me lately—helping me figure out how to close the deal on that property I want. Did he tell you?" She bustled about the kitchen, not waiting for an answer. "Sit down, and have some coffee."

An angel or an opportunist? Alexis kept her thoughts to herself as she pulled out a barstool at the counter and sat. "Yeah, he mentioned it."

Oma opened the fridge and riffled around. "Do you want some bacon?"

"Definitely." Alexis took a sip of coffee. Maybe it would be best to head off any talk about her romantic life by asking Oma about the camp she wanted to buy. "So, Oma ... tell me about this real estate deal you're working on. Have you signed anything yet?"

Oma put a plate of buttered toast in front of Alexis. "I'll have the bacon for you in a minute. Do you want some eggs, too?"

"Yes, please." Alexis usually skipped breakfast, but she knew Oma enjoyed cooking for her.

"The camp is pretty much a done deal, thanks to Justin. Let me take you there today!" Oma smiled. "I have so many ideas to make it beautiful."

Alexis felt a pang of guilt in her gut as she watched Oma's face light up. The camp obviously meant a great deal to her. Who was she to spoil the fun? Except, what if this fun led to Oma working herself to the bone and living in poverty during her retirement years? And now, with her own job gone, she couldn't be much help—at least not financially.

Oma cracked an egg into the frying pan. "Now, enough about me, dear. Tell me, what happened with you and Nick?"

There it was.

"We broke up last Christmas. I'm sorry I didn't tell you earlier. I guess I was ashamed. I didn't want to let you down. We decided to continue working as partners with the YouTube channel because it was doing so well. Companies were depending on us and we had contracts to fulfill."

Alexis picked at her toast and took a buttery bite. Oma added bacon and eggs to the plate, then sat down. Her grandmother nodded, her face expressing compassion and understanding.

"That must have been hard."

"It was. A few days ago, we were shooting a video for a Christmas campaign at a resort in Colorado. It was supposed to seem romantic and dreamy. The fakery was over-the-top ridiculous." Alexis gave a wry laugh. "We both felt it, but I guess that was the final straw for Nick. He told me he was done pretending before taking off to Seattle, leaving me to clean up the mess with all our clients."

"That fink!" Oma shook her head with a look of disgust on her face.

Alexis smiled, amused at her grandmother's word choice. At least someone was on her side. "Believe me, I agree with you. Though, if I'd had a job lined up for myself, I can't say I wouldn't have done the same thing."

"Yes, well, I might have something for you regarding a job. I can't say it's as glamorous as jetting around the world and getting paid to make YouTube videos for a living, but I could use your help with the camp."

Taking a sip of coffee, Alexis did her best to stall on what to say next. How could she be diplomatic? Oma was only trying to help.

"Oma—I—"

"Don't give me your answer yet. Let me take you there and show you around. I know you have your doubts about this whole thing, but wait until you see it. Justin is meeting me there this morning with some papers to sign." Oma took a sip of coffee. "But let's not concern ourselves with that now. What I want to know is how you're doing. How's your heart?"

Dear Oma, she never was one to shy away from deep talks. "I'm fine, Oma. I don't have a broken heart. I promise. Strangely, I feel a little … relieved. Nick isn't the man for me. We're just friends—or we were. Now, I'm not so sure. But I have a lot of work I need to do today. Do you mind if I hold off on going to the camp until later this week?"

Oma nodded in agreement, but the flash of disappointment in her eyes told Alexis something different. She needed to make those phone calls. Extricating herself from those remaining commitments with her clients was a task that hung over Alexis like a black cloud. But those papers Oma planned on signing? What was in them? There was only one way to find out.

"Actually, on second thought, I'll go with you. What time did you say we needed to leave?"

***

Justin awoke early to get to Pangborn Airport and retrieve his truck before anyone in town saw him driving around in the ridiculous orange Fiat. The sooner he returned that car, the better.

Without that storm, he might not have had his encounter with Alexis Jacobson in Seattle, so it hadn't been all bad. Offering her a ride home had been the right thing to do, but when had he ever enjoyed a long car ride so much? Of course, Alexis had a boyfriend, so it would be best to put her out of his head and focus on other matters—like the meeting he had later today with Clarice Jacobson, Alexis's grandmother.

Justin's mind wandered over the last few days. His time in DC had gone well and the National Register of Historic Places had accepted his grant proposal. Clarice would be the first beneficiary. He couldn't wait to give her the good news.

After last night's rainstorm, the valley sparkled in the early morning light. Now that his condo in DC was finally sold, Justin's return to small-town living was complete. Driving past the park with its white gazebo and the old-world, alpine-style buildings adorned with geranium-filled window boxes, Justin thought about what his friend Mike said at dinner the other night. Mike worked for a popular travel website that was sponsoring a contest called America's Favorite Christmastown.

Icicle Creek could be a strong contender, and winning would bring great publicity. The boost it would bring to the local economy would be significant—not just benefitting his own business, but others' as well. Justin decided he'd present the opportunity at tonight's town council meeting to and gauge people's interest. An undertaking like this would require everyone to pitch in.

Justin pressed his foot down on the gas pedal to accelerate as soon as he passed the last building on Main Street. He might look silly in this car, but it was zippy—and kind of fun to drive.

An hour later, after returning the rental and retrieving his truck, he took the turn off Highway 2 at Cole's Corner and headed toward Lake Haven Retreat Center. Would Alexis be with Clarice today? And why was he still thinking about Alexis? Put her out of your mind, dude, he chastised himself.

The final stretch of gravel road toward Lake Haven's main lodge meandered past five log cabins that featured broken windows and concealed pathways Nature was slowly taking over from years of neglect, giving the buildings an aura of mystery.

The camp had seen better days. Justin remembered staying in cabin three for winter camp when he was ten. Back then, the place had felt magical. Sledding, ice-fishing, eating those delicious cheddar biscuits the camp cook made, and shooting the breeze with friends around the dining hall's fireplace each night—those memories made Justin nostalgic for how it used to be.

Helping Mrs. Jacobson find a way to bring Lake Haven Retreat Center back to its former glory had been one of the first projects he'd undertaken since he'd returned to Icicle Creek and opened his real estate business. He wanted to give back to his community. The slower pace of life here gave him the time to do more of that. Telling the sweet old lady that her dream of restoring Lake Haven Retreat Center could begin was going to be immensely gratifying.

Mrs. Jacobson's Jeep was already parked in front of the lodge. As Justin parked his truck next to it, he spotted her with Alexis. They were on the wrap-around porch, peering through the dirty windows into the empty building. Alexis wore khaki shorts that showed off her long, suntanned legs, and her hair was pulled into a ponytail. She looked beautiful. There was no denying it. When the two ladies noticed him, he got out of the truck, raised his hand, and waved. "I've got some good news for you!"

Clarice gave an enthusiastic whoop, but Alexis, furrowed her brow, and crossed her arms in front of her chest. He recalled their conversation last night, and how it had stalled and her tone had chilled after he'd mentioned working with her grandmother on the purchase of the property. Now he was starting to get the picture.

Alexis wasn't happy about her grandmother buying this camp. Not at all.

CHAPTER FOUR

Alexis followed Oma and Justin down the over-grown path behind the lodge toward the lake, noting her grandmother's careful steps, along with the considerate way Justin matched his pace to hers, offering an arm for support when-ever the downward slope was particularly steep.

Oma's eightieth birthday was coming up in August, although anyone who didn't know oth-erwise would probably guess she was at least twenty years younger. Her spunk, vivacious-ness, and youthful flair for the current fashions could fool just about anyone. Today she wore blue jeans, a t-shirt, and tennies, along with a giant pair of fuchsia statement earrings. Her hair, a lovely shade of silver, was cut in an asymmetrical bob, and while there were a few smile lines around her mouth and eyes, her skin had the luminous glow of someone who enjoyed plenty of fresh air and exercise. But Alexis knew Oma wasn't invincible to the effects of aging. Over her last few visits, she'd noticed the small changes creeping into her grandmother's daily routines: the naps, the growing collection of daily medications, and the overall slowing down. A protective instinct told her to keep Oma safe and do her best to help eliminate any additional sources of stress in her grandmother's life.

They didn't have any other family, and Alexis knew their roles were beginning to reverse. Oma needed her. It was her turn to care for the woman who so lovingly stepped in as a surrogate mother when Alexis had no one else.

A view of the sparkling, clear-blue lake appeared as Alexis turned a bend in the path. Though it was only ten in the morning, the heat was intense. She remembered with fondness, first learning how to swim in this lake, but Alexis wasn't here to reminisce. She was here to put a stop to this madness.

Alexis could concede that the camp had loads of potential and possessed a certain rustic charm, but as her eyes moved toward the rotting wood dock, all she saw were dollar signs and many hours of intense manual labor. Why did Oma want to take on this headache? Who buys a vacation business at the age of eighty?

Justin's announcement about how he'd secured some type of grant to help Oma pay for the camp had only made everything harder for Alexis. Oma's over-the-top enthusiasm was almost contagious, but Alexis remained firm in her resolve. Today was no time to be swayed by emotion. So far, they'd toured the main lodge—essentially a large, open room for dining, complete with a crumbling fireplace, and a kitchen. Then they'd toured one of the decrepit cabins with broken windows. Oh, and the outhouse. Only the main lodge had indoor plumbing.

What was in this deal for Justin? Why was he going out of his way to help secure a grant for Oma? Of course, there would probably be a hefty commission in it for him. But even if his motives were pure, and he really did just want to help Oma, he probably didn't realize how old she actually was—or how much work was required to get this camp up and running as a business. Alexis was more realistic. Was Justin the upstanding guy he seemed to be or had his time in DC changed him into a power-hungry investor? Alexis aimed to find out.

As they exited the woods, Oma gave an excited squeal. "There's a boathouse, too?" She rushed over to the windows to peer inside. "And there's a canoe in there!"

Alexis joined her grandmother at the surprisingly intact window. A memory of canoeing on this lake with her best friend, Katrin, floated to the surface. "I wonder if that's the same canoe I went out in when I was a camper here?"

Oma took Alexis's hand and squeezed it. "Justin, this is simply perfect. How long do you think it will take before we can get started on the improvements here? I want it to be ready for the Christmas season."

"If you sign the papers today, you should have the keys in about four weeks, tops."

"Uh, Oma...before you sign anything, I want to talk to you first," Alexis interrupted.

"Sure, honey." Oma responded. Turning to Justin, she gave an apologetic smile. "I'm going to take my granddaughter out to lunch. We'll talk, and then I'll swing by your office. Will you be available this afternoon?"

"Of course. Is there anything else you'd like to see before we go?"

"Let's check out cabin three. I haven't seen that one yet."

They walked back up the hill, did a jaunt to the right of the lodge, and were soon standing at the door of cabin three.

"I think we could do better with the names on these buildings, don't you?" Oma mused as she waited for Justin to unlock the door.

As the door opened and a whoosh of moving air hit her face, Alexis ducked in horror at the accompanying sound of wings flapping and high-pitched squeaks. Bats! She ran towards Oma's Jeep and jumped in, quickly closing the door behind her. Oma, unfazed, took her time perusing the cabin.

After chatting a bit longer with Justin on the porch, Oma shook his hand. What were they saying? Justin glanced toward the car where she was waiting. He gave a quick wave with a smile before getting into his truck. She returned it with a half-hearted wave. When Oma returned to the Jeep, Alexis had a suggestion. "We could call that cabin "The Bat Cave."

***

Antonio's had the best views of any restaurant in town. Outside, a ridge of mountains served as a dramatic backdrop to Icicle Creek. Even in July, snow remained on some of the highest peaks. Alexis glanced at the menu. The butternut squash ravioli was her favorite, which Oma knew. Was bringing her here an attempt to soften her up?

"Alexis, before you say anything, I want to put your mind at ease," Oma said, foregoing any small talk. "I've put a lot of thought into buying

Lake Haven Retreat Center, and I promise you, it makes sense. I anticipate this becoming not only a fun business for me, but a great investment as well. But I know you have concerns, so go ahead; ask me anything you want."

Alexis put down her menu. "Okay, start at the beginning. What's your vision for the place?"

"I've been watching your YouTube channel these past few years, and the places you visit made me realize that Icicle Creek is just as beautiful as any of those far-flung locales you go to, but not many people know about it yet. And, as you may recall, I enjoy a good renovation project. The camp is just one of those, but on a bigger scale." Oma gave a satisfied smile, pausing her pitch so the waitress could take their order

After the waitress left, Oma continued. "Once I add some paint, new flooring, lighting, furniture, kitchenettes, and bathrooms to each cabin, I'll offer them as short-term vacation rentals. We can use the lodge for wedding receptions! And the property is glorious, isn't it? So many people from this community have fond memories of going to camp at Lake Haven Retreat Center."

"Yes, but Oma, when you offer vacation rentals, you need to attract customers from outside the community. Since the camp's location is off the beaten path, you'll need to do a lot of marketing to get the word out."

"Exactly, dear!" Oma smiled and took Alexis's hand. "That's where you come in."

"I want to help you, Oma. I do. But I'm only here for a little while until I figure out what to do next with my career. I can't stay in Icicle Creek forever."

"You won't have to. Once we get everything up and running, you can help me find someone to take your place."

It wasn't as if her grandmother didn't know how to run a business. The woman had run a successful clothing boutique just a few doors down the street until just a few years ago.

Oma had thought this through more than Alexis had given her credit for. She felt her resolve begin to weaken. "I admire your ambition, Oma, and it does sound like a good plan. But what's the rush? Do you really need to sign the papers today?"

"Well, I told Justin I would go by his office after lunch, and I'm anxious to get started. I don't want to lose out on anything."

"I would feel so much better if I could talk to Justin and look over the papers before you sign anything. Would you be okay with that?"

"If it makes you feel better, then sure. Okay."

"Thank you," Alexis said, noting the flicker of disappointment that crossed Oma's face. "It really is a beautiful property," she continued softly. "I just want to make sure there won't be any surprises."

Just then, the waitress arrived with the mouthwatering plates of food, offering Alexis a welcome distraction.

After a few minutes of quietly enjoying their meal, Oma smiled and spoke again. "So, tell me about your ride home last night with Justin. Did you enjoy spending time with him? Everyone around here is so happy he moved back to Icicle Creek."

Oh, no. No, no, no. Oma's projects usually fell into two categories: decorating and matchmaking. A true romantic at heart, Oma was a frequent guest at weddings because she was often credited with having introduced the bride and groom. . Alexis knew where this line of questioning was going, and she was not interested. "It was fine, Oma, but please...don't be getting any ideas."

Oma put down her fork and moved her features into her most innocent expression. "Of course not, honey."

***

Justin finished the last of his turkey bagel sandwich and, as he tossed the paper wrapping in the trash, realized his office now smelled like onions. That wouldn't do; Alexis would be arriving any minute. He went to the window and opened it, letting in some fresh air.

Mrs. Jacobson had called him an hour ago to apologize, telling him she wouldn't be able to come by the office this afternoon after all—but she wanted to send her granddaughter instead. "She has some questions, and I'm sure you'll be able to set her mind at ease," she'd concluded.

As he thought about his next meeting, Justin watched what was happening on the street below. Gina Pauly was setting out a water bowl for any dogs who might pass by the bookshop. Farther down the block, Tom Clark, the sheriff, was chatting with Hank on the sidewalk outside Hank's Hardware. After being in DC for several years, Justin had a renewed appreciation for this place. Icicle Creek was the kind of town where neighbors looked out for each other.

Justin hoped he'd be able to convince Alexis that he was looking out for her grandmother. Alexis's posture that morning had demonstrated she didn't trust him and those bats were an unwelcome surprise that had sent her running. It might have been funny if she hadn't been so genuinely scared. He'd have to be on his A-game with her.

Justin returned to his desk and opened his laptop. The sooner Clarice signed those papers, the better. He would hate to see someone else swoop in and buy the place while his client was still deliberating. It would break her heart to lose out on the deal. Not to mention that he, too, needed to start making some sales—soon—if he planned to stay in Icicle Creek.

A light rap on the door signaled she was here. If Alexis wanted to challenge him, he was ready. Game on.

CHAPTER FIVE

"Hey Justin, thanks for meeting me." Alexis's gaze moved around the small office as she stood in the doorway. The large window that viewed Main Street was its best asset. Otherwise, it was a generic room containing a desk, two chairs, a bookshelf, and one potted palm—all of it, recognizably, from Ikea. He was a minimalist, she observed, but she couldn't surmise much else about the room's occupant.

Justin glanced up from his screen and smiled. "Hey, Alexis. No problem. Come on in."

Alexis stepped further into the room. "So, how has is been for you being back in Icicle Creek?"

"I'm still settling in, but it's good to be back. Please," Justin motioned to a chair in front of his desk. "Have a seat. Your grandmother said you had some questions about the property? I'll be happy to answer them as best I can."

Alexis decided to get straight to the point. "I have some concerns about what purchasing a property like Lake Haven Retreat Center might do to my grandmother. The grant you helped her apply for is wonderful—and it does help alleviate some of the financial pressure—but I believe there are still some issues at hand that you might not be aware of. She respects you, so I thought she might be more willing to listen if a voice of reason came from you."

"Uh, huh..." Justin's expression remained neutral.

"Do you know she's turning eighty next month? I know everything probably looks good on paper, but...." Alexis leaned back and gave a deep sigh. Hearing those words come from her own mouth gave her pause. Did she really want to convince Justin to see her side of things? What if she was wrong? Maybe she was under-estimating Oma.

Justin's eyebrows shot up. "Eighty? Wow! I would never have guessed. Your grandmother is a remarkable woman." He offered a gentle smile. "I can go over this paperwork with you— show you the numbers and everything." He opened a drawer, pulled out a file, and then pushed it across the desk toward Alexis.

Alexis opened the file and found a large stack of papers. She followed along, reading and listening for the next few minutes as Justin patiently went through the offer with her. When they got to the last page, Alexis was convinced that, indeed, Oma was getting a steal of a deal, but she still had concerns.

"Thank you, Justin." She paused. "My grandmother doesn't have any other family around—besides me. And I know it's not your job to get involved in personal matters like this, but I'm just trying to protect her. I don't want to see Oma burdened with a business that's more than she can handle on her own."

Justin closed the file and then leaned back in his chair. He seemed to be thinking carefully about his next words. "The cafe downstairs is more comfortable than my office. Do you want to continue the conversation there? Please, let me buy you a cup of coffee."

"Oh? Well, okay. I appreciate you taking the time."

"My pleasure." He seemed sincere.

A friendly voice from behind the front counter greeted her.

"Alexis! Hey, good to see you! When did you get back in town?" Oma's neighbor, Doris, walked around the counter to welcome Alexis with a hug.

"It's good to see you, too, Doris. I arrived last night." Alexis looked around, admiring the cozy ambiance of the café. "Is this your shop?"

"Nah, I just work here. This place belongs to my son, Jack. What can I get for you?"

After ordering—an iced vanilla latte for Alexis and a plain drip coffee for Justin—they took a table in a quiet corner.

Alexis nodded toward Doris, who was now helping another customer. "It has been so long since I lived here. I almost forgot how great it feels to be greeted by familiar faces when I'm out and about."

Justin's eyes wandered around the room, and he nodded in agreement. "Yeah, this town is something special. People help each other out here." He took a sip of coffee. "So, now that we've gone over the financial details of Lake Haven Retreat Center, let's talk about the other concerns you have."

"Well, I mean ... it's a big place, and there's a ton of work to do. Can this town really support another vacation rental business?"

"True, there's a lot of work to be done, but I think you might be underestimating how much support she has in this community. She won't be on her own. As for sustainability, it's true we already have a few hotels, two Bed-and-Breakfast establishments, and a handful of AirBnBs, but tourism has been picking up over the last few years. I believe there's a need for more lodging."

Over the next hour, Alexis and Justin discussed, in detail, everything from the local business climate to construction logistics and timelines—as well as the requirements that went with registering Lake Haven as a historical site and securing the grant. He had an answer for everything. She wanted to believe what Justin was saying was true: Oma would take ownership of Lake Haven, which would benefit both her grandmother and Icicle Creek.

Alexis realized she'd lost track of time when Doris wandered over to their table with two chocolate croissants. "A little treat for the both of you, on the house ... just my way of saying 'welcome home.'"

Alexis smiled. "That's very sweet of you, Doris. Thank you." The croissants smelled terrific.

Doris smiled and waved her hand as if it was nothing, then walked away to greet another group of people as they entered the cafe.

Alexis bit into the decadent pastry and considered how the entire afternoon had gone differently from what she had expected. She'd been prepared for something more confrontational or unpleasant. But instead, she'd been disarmed by Justin's kindness. He'd remained steadfast in his commitment to champion Oma's cause, and now, Alexis wanted nothing more than some time to herself. She needed to think. It wasn't easy to admit when she might be wrong. And she wasn't going to—not yet, anyway.

Justin wiped the crumbs from the last of his croissant off his fingers. "That was delicious. Hey, I've got to get going, but before I do, I wanted to let you know that there's a town council meeting tonight at seven. I'm presenting about a Christmas contest that I hope to get people excited about. You should bring your grandmother. She might like to get involved."

Alexis couldn't believe it when she heard herself saying, "Sure, I'll be there."

Justin had some strange kind of magical persuasive powers, Alexis concluded. She would need to be much stronger—for Oma.

***

Justin hurried to his truck after saying goodbye to Alexis. He had another client meeting across town in five minutes. The afternoon had gotten away from him in the most agreeable way possible, despite being grilled.

He couldn't fault Alexis for being cautious. The purchase of Lake Haven was a big undertaking. Clarice Jacobson was lucky to have such a strong advocate in her corner.

As he drove, Justin let his mind wander to how enjoyable it would be to spend more time with Alexis. She was intelligent, ambitious, and attractive. And she lit up a room with her beautiful smile. Where was her boyfriend ... what was his name? Nick? Why wasn't he here right now?

Pulling up to a stop sign, Justin checked the address on his phone. Yep, as he thought, this property was right on the river within five minutes of town—a prime location. He turned right and drove down a long gravel driveway amid dense woods, until he reached the end of the road, where a clear view of the Wenatchee River revealed itself at the foot of the mountains. A small log cabin sat like a jewel box in the center of this scene.

Justin smiled as he put the truck in park. This property was going to be easy to sell. It was just the kind of place he would choose for himself. Don't get ahead of yourself. Get your business established first. The apartment is okay for now.

Justin turned off the engine and got out. Ben Mangle, waiting in the front yard, gave a friendly wave in greeting.

"Nice place you've got here." Justin offered a hand. "Justin Karon."

"Good to meet you, and thank you," Ben said, accepting the handshake with a firm grip. "Yeah, it won't be easy to part with. My wife and I have lived here near thirty-five years, but it's time to move closer to family. The grandkids are in Phoenix, and we don't want to miss out. They grow up so fast." Ben paused and looked Justin in the eye. "Are you Mayor Karon's son?"

"Sure am."

"That's all I need to know. Your mother is a good woman, and I trust the apple doesn't fall far from the tree. Can you help me sell this place?"

"Yes, I can do that. Let's take a look around."

An hour later, Justin was back in his truck, heading home with a new listing. The Mangle property would go fast, as the owners were mo-tivated to sell and it was move-in ready. The in-side of the two-bedroom cabin had been well cared for over the years. It wasn't fancy, but it was warm and welcoming, with many built-ins and handcrafted touches. Whoever ended up with this house would be very lucky, indeed.

It was five o'clock already—just enough time to go home, grab something to eat, and get ready for that evening's town council meeting.

CHAPTER SIX

When Alexis arrived at the house, Oma was working in her front garden. Alexis wandered over and plopped down on the warm grass. The older woman continued clipping away at some overgrown rose bushes. "How'd it go, honey? Did you get your questions answered?"

"I feel better than I did before." Alexis paused. "Are you sure this is what you want, Oma?"

"Oh, yes. Just thinking about what I can do with the Lake Haven property makes me happy. I think it will be a good project for both of us."

Alexis smiled. "I'm not ready to commit yet, as far as how long or how much I can be around to help, but I promise you, I'll give it some serious thought. When do you need my answer?"

Oma took off her gardening gloves and turned to face Alexis. "You've helped me already. You encouraged me to slow down enough to look at all sides of this plan. You're a smart cookie—always have been. At this time in my life, I believe the most prudent way to buy this property is to do it with a business partner. Without one, I'll pass—so that's what I'm offering you—a partnership. I'll put up the money for the purchase and remodel, but then we go 50/50 as soon as we start bringing in some cash. What do you think?" Oma leaned back on her heels and took off her gardening gloves. Before Alexis could answer, Oma continued, "It's a big decision—I know—but this property won't stay on the market forever. Can you give me an answer by tomorrow?"

"Yes, but can we talk more tonight, over dinner? Right now, I need to go inside and catch up on some emails. Alexis looked closer at Oma and noticed her flushed face. "Do you want me to bring you a glass of lemonade?"

"That would be perfect, dear. Thank you."

A few minutes later, as Alexis was handing her grandmother a glass of lemonade, she remembered the meeting. "Do you want to go to the town council meeting tonight? Justin wants to get people on board with some big plan he has ... a Christmas contest or something."

"Ah, yes. I was already planning on it."

Oma's answer didn't surprise Alexis. Icicle Creek residents regularly attended council meetings. Alexis had tagged along with Oma to a few of them back in high school, and knew that a lively discussion could always be expected—as well as a tray of home-baked cookies.

Alexis grabbed her laptop and went into Oma's sunroom, mentally preparing herself for the tasks ahead. She'd already written to several clients, explaining the necessity of canceling their upcoming collaborations, but offered forth the idea of coming alone—without Nick. Of course, there was little chance any of them would take her up on that idea, but it was worth a shot.

Opening her email, Alexis could see she already had several responses. She clicked on the one from the resort in Puerta Vallarta first. They were, understandably, unhappy, and the company was seeking monetary damages for breach of contract. Alexis forwarded that one to Nick. She proceeded to pass several more along to him as well. Before long, her head hurt. None of their clients were interested in working with her, alone. It was Alexis and Nick, or nothing. She and Nick had been selling a false reality, and now it had come back to bite them.

Next, Alexis opened up her editing program. She still had to edit the Colorado Christmas footage—it would be the last of the Nick and Alexis videos. This sponsored vlog wouldn't be scheduled to go live for several more months, but Alexis wanted to get it over with and move on. Good riddance.

She hit play and watched herself on the screen, playing the part of a woman in love, snuggled on the couch in front of a fireplace in a cozy Christmas scene. I should have been an actress. Both she and Nick had executed their roles to perfection. She felt like a fraud. What do I even know of love?

An hour later, Alexis closed her computer. She still had more work to do, but her headache made it hard to think straight, and it was time for dinner.

***

After their meal, Alexis and Oma decided to walk to the town hall meeting since it was a warm summer evening and their destination was close by. Mayor Karon greeted them in the lobby when they arrived. Justin's mother had been mayor for as long as Alexis could remember. "Hello, Clarice—and Alexis, how good to see you! I thought I'd heard you were home." Mayor Karon held out her arms, offering a hug instead of a handshake.

There didn't seem to be a thing that happened in Icicle Creek that Mayor Karon didn't know about. "Hey, Mayor Karon. It's good to be back." Alexis accepted the warm hug with a smile.

"I hope I brought enough cookies. Looks like quite a crowd tonight." Oma gave a satisfied nod of approval as she glanced through the open doorway into the main hall, where people had filled nearly every chair.

"Here, I can take those for you. Go on, get yourselves some seats before they're all gone." Mayor Karon took the plate of chocolate chip cookies from Oma and walked away to set them on a table in the back of the room that was already filled with an array of baked goods.

Alexis spotted Justin across the room, sitting next to his older sister, Elyse. An adorable little girl, no more than six, sat on his lap. The little girl, who wore her dark hair in pigtails, looked a lot like Elyse. Was she Justin's niece? Justin glanced up at that moment. She felt her cheeks grow warm as she waved at him, embarrassed that he'd caught her staring.

Mayor Karon walked to the front of the room and called the meeting to order. After a brief discussion on whether the city would have the gazebo repainted this year, the council voted, and it passed. Then they opened the floor to community members. Justin stood and walked to the podium.

"I'd like to tell you all about an opportunity for our community to get some valuable publicity, which would bring in additional tourism for the holiday season in years to come," he announced. A murmur among the people in the room affirmed that Justin had their attention. "American Travel.com sponsors a contest called America's Favorite Christmastown. They will feature the winning town on their website and on several nationally televised news programs. The entries will be judged on aesthetics, community spirit, hospitality, and an overall feeling of Christmas. I think we can do this, but we'll need the whole community to pitch in to help make it happen. I'm willing to head it up if this is what you all want to do, but I'll need your help."

Alexis had to admit that Icicle Creek seemed like a shoo-in for winning the title. With its millions of twinkly holiday lights, the Bavarian-themed buildings, and abundant snow every winter, the Christmas season in Icicle Creek resembled the mythical North Pole—or at least the set of a holiday movie.

From the back of the room, a gruff voice belonging to Fred Olson rang out. "We don't need any more publicity. Why would we want more folks visiting? We're already at capacity!"

Floris Hofstetter, who operated a bed-and breakfast on Main Street, stood. "You've got my support, Justin. I think it's a great idea!"

Fortunately for Justin, Fred's opinion was in the minority. Several more people stood after that, offering support and asking questions.

Alexis couldn't deny that Lake Haven Retreat Center would benefit from the kind of publicity this contest might bring. She began to imagine what the camp would look like with fairy lights strung through the trees and a giant Christmas tree in the main lodge. The big fireplace would be a cozy gathering spot for families and friends. Fluffy down comforters in the cabins, groomed trails for cross-country skiing … her ideas began to snowball until Alexis shook her thoughts loose and returned to the present. Where did all that come from? Am I really going to do this?

Alexis put her hand over Oma's and gave it a little squeeze. When Oma turned her way, she nodded and mouthed the words. "Yes. Let's do this!"

CHAPTER SEVEN

The whiff of burnt rubber grew stronger as Justin drove out to Lake Haven Retreat Center. After parking in front of the lodge, he popped the hood of his truck and peered at the engine. He wasn't much of a mechanic, but that horrible smell seemed to signal a problem.

Hopefully, his truck would make it safely back to town because, unfortunately, there were no Ubers in Icicle Creek. Town was only five miles away, but the August sun was already blazing hot, and Justin didn't have time to walk. An hour from now, he was supposed to meet with Ben Mangle to present an offer that had just come in for his cabin from a property developer out of Arizona. It was a good offer. Too bad Justin wanted nothing more than to rip it up. He was sure the developer would bulldoze the cabin in order to build something bigger, but his duty to Mr. Mangle was to present all reasonable offers and let his client decide what to do with them. Justin reminded himself that his feelings had no place getting in the way of business. He'd like to buy the home for himself, but wasn't the right time, and besides, he couldn't beat the price this developer was offering.

When he saw Clarice Jacobson's Jeep approaching, Justin closed the hood on his truck and resolved to put his problems out of mind. He was here to hand over the keys for the camp to his favorite client. After a month of waiting, the deal had finally closed. Lake Haven belonged to the Jacobsons. Today was a day to celebrate.

When the car got closer, Justin saw that Alexis was with her grandmother. She'd been in Icicle Creek for a month, but there was still no sign of her boyfriend. What did that mean? Was he still in the picture?

Mrs. Jacobson parked next to the truck and excitedly leaped out of her car. "The day is finally here! You've got my keys?"

Justin laughed and handed them over. "It has been an honor to help you throughout this process. Thank you for trusting me with your business."

Alexis, standing next to her grandmother, offered a smile. "Thank you, Justin."

Clarice put her hand on his arm. "You've been wonderful, Justin. Thank you. I'll be sure to recommend you to anyone I know who needs a real estate agent." She paused, then threw her arms up. "Well, it's all ours now, Alexis! Let's get to work."

Justin felt a pang of regret that he had to leave—for several reasons. "I have to get going now. But please, let me know if there's anything I can do to help. Also, give me a call if you need an extra hand with the heavy lifting."

The women waved goodbye and then entered the main lodge together. Justin returned to his truck. Thankfully, it started.

***

Alexis took notes as she followed her grandmother around the property. The list of needed improvements was extensive. They'd need to prioritize. Removing the bats from cabin three was number one on the list. Who should they call for that?

Oma, who'd been pulling weeds away from the front porch of the main lodge, stopped and brushed the dirt from her hands. "Alexis, I'm starting to get hungry. Maybe we should go back into town and get some lunch. If I'd been thinking clearly, I'd have picked something up on the way. I'd really rather stay here and work. There isn't any time to waste."

"If you want to stay here, I can get some lunch for us and bring it back. Does a sub sandwich from Ernie's sound okay? Turkey and avocado on whole wheat?"

"You remember my favorite sandwich? Yes, that would be lovely. Thank you, dear. I left the keys in the ignition."

"You got it." She'd warned Oma about leaving the keys in the ignition before. It wasn't the safest thing to do. But some habits never changed, and Alexis had to admit that crime wasn't much of a problem in Icicle Creek.

Borrowing Oma's car was fine for now, but purchasing a ride of her own would also need to go on the to-do list. She'd have to dip into her savings.

Alexis was only a mile down Pine Tree Road when she saw Justin's truck pulled off to the side, with Justin standing beside it, talking on his phone. The hood was up, and there was smoke coming from under it. As Alexis slowed down and parked behind the truck, Justin put the phone in his pocket and walked toward her. It looked like it was her turn to return the favor of a ride.

"Do you have another ride on the way? Or do you want me to drive you into town?"

"Actually, I could use a ride. Thank you! You don't mind?"

"Of course not. Hop in. Where do you need me to drop you off?"

"Do you know the Mangle place? By the river?"

"I don't think so. Just tell me the directions."

Justin looked surprisingly calm, given the circumstances. Alexis waved her hand towards the back seat. "There's some bottled water on the floor behind your seat if you're thirsty. I'm sorry about your truck. I hope it's not too serious."

"She's a temperamental thing, but I'm sure she'll be up and running again soon. I was just on the phone with Bob's Towing. He'll take a look at it for me, but he's twenty miles away, and I have a meeting in a few minutes. I appreciate your timing. I thought I was going to have to walk back."

"No problem. I was just on my way to get some lunch."

Once they were well on their way, the conversation turned toward the Christmas contest. Justin became more animated as he talked. "We need to submit a video entry to the committee, and I know that's your area of expertise. If you want to be involved...."

"Whatever you need. I would love to help." The words flew out of Alexis's mouth before she realized what she was committing herself to. What am I doing? It was too late to take it back.

"Really?" Justin smiled. "That's awesome. I'll take you up on that. Do you want to get dinner together tonight? You know. To talk about it."

Alexis pushed away a question that made her face grow warm. Was this a dinner about her civic involvement or something more? "Dinner? Uh, sure. Do you want me to pick you up? Since, you know, your truck...."

CHAPTER EIGHT

Alexis riffled through her closet, searching for something suitable to wear to dinner with Justin. After several years of living out of a suitcase, having a closet to herself felt like a luxury. She pulled out a short black sundress and studied it. Too flirty. Her blue floral shift? It looked like she was trying too hard. Finally, Alexis settled on a sleeveless blue chambray shirt with white denim shorts and sandals. It would have to do.

"I won't be gone long," Alexis called out to Oma as she left the house.

"Take your time. I'll be fine." Oma stood in the hallway and made a shooing motion with her hands. Like a cat that ate the canary, Oma wasn't hiding her pleasure over Alexis's dinner plans with Justin, and it didn't matter how much Alexis insisted it was nothing more than business.

"Bye, Oma."

"Goodbye. Take a sweater. It gets chilly in the evenings."

Alexis grabbed a cardigan hanging by the front door and stuffed it in her leather tote. Der Pizza Haus was a quick two-block walk from the house. She wondered where Justin lived, thinking it couldn't be far since he hadn't needed a ride. She'd spent many hours at Der Pizza Haus in high school. It was a local hangout with live music, bright lights, loud conversations, and a slightly grungy appearance, but it served up the best deep-dish pizza she'd ever had. . It hardly seemed the ideal place to discuss the video they'd be working on together, but she was going along with it. Maybe it had changed.

Alexis double-checked the sign above the door when she got there. Was she at the right place? If this was Der Pizza Haus, the restaurant had undergone quite the makeover. Stepping inside, she was greeted with moody lighting, a cozy ambiance, and soft music.

When Justin walked in, he seemed to note her confusion. "New owners. But the pizza is still as good as ever." His blue eyes focused on hers and he smiled. "Hey."

Alexis felt her cheeks growing warm and averted her eyes. She didn't want Justin to know the effect he had on her. "Hey. Well, good to know because it's my favorite pizza. The place looks great."

A young girl ushered them toward the only open table. Justin pulled out Alexis's chair for her, a move she considered quaint and sweet. Der Pizza Haus might have changed, but Justin was the same guy she had carried a crush on all those years ago. *Remember why you're here.* After ordering the Sicilian special, Alexis reached into her tote and pulled out her laptop. "I had some ideas for the video."

Justin took notes as Alexis outlined a plan. It felt like a welcome return to normalcy. She was in her element again, for the first time in more than a month. Video production was what she was good at. But it was also a reminder of the mess she had made for herself.

When the pizza came, Alexis put away her laptop and savored every bit of mouth-watering goodness when she took the first cheesy bite. Justin smiled, clearly amused by the way she was enjoying her food. "This pizza was my first meal when I moved back from DC There's nothing like it."

Alexis agreed. "I forgot to ask. Did you get any news today on your truck?"

"Yeah, it was a broken hose. Bob already made the repairs. Hey, thanks again for the ride earlier. You're an angel."

The conversation about the Christmas contest and their video entry was forgotten for the next few minutes as Alexis began to let down her guard and share more about what brought her back to Icicle Creek. "Nick and I broke up a long time ago. We were pretending to be a couple for the YouTube channel." There. It was out.

People would know soon enough, anyway. It was better this way. If he wanted nothing to do with her after this, it was better to get it over with. Alexis watched Justin's expression for any sign of judgment. He was hard to read. At that moment, his phone buzzed, breaking his attention away from her. As he read the text message, he set his jaw and furrowed his brow.

"I'm so sorry, Alexis. It's a work emergency. I have to go."

Was it really an emergency? Or had her disclosure scared him away? Alexis had a sinking feeling in the pit of her stomach.

***

Alexis opened the bag of coffee beans and inhaled. So what if it was nine in the evening? She planned to work late tonight and finish the video production plan she'd promised Justin. It would take her one step closer to fulfilling her commitment and being done with it. The sooner it was over, the better. Seeing him again would be awkward, working with him even more so. That was the trouble with small towns. It was impossible to avoid people. She riffled through the cupboard until she found the coffee grinder. Success. The sound of beans grinding under the blade was oddly satisfying.

There was no one else to be irritated with but herself. Why wouldn't Justin think poorly of her? The duplicity she took part in was inexcusable. If I were in his shoes, I'd run for the door, too. Alexis was embarrassed and ashamed. But she was also annoyed with Justin. It had been rude, the way he'd bailed on her.

She let out a sigh as she dumped the coffee into the filter. Justin hadn't wasted any time getting up from the table after she'd told him the truth about herself and Nick. The text had been too convenient. Sure, he'd made some excuse about a work emergency and kindly paid the bill before leaving, but it was clear he didn't want to have anything to do with her. Too bad. The evening had started off so well.

Alexis hit the start button on the coffee machine just as Oma wandered into the kitchen.

"Coffee? It's late, dear. How are you ever going to get to sleep?"

"I've got some work to do so it's going to be a late night. Don't worry; I'll be out like a light as soon as my head hits the pillow."

"How was dinner?"

Alexis turned away, knowing Oma could read her better than anyone else. She did her best to keep her voice neutral. "Good. Der Pizza Haus went through quite a makeover, but I'm glad they kept the same menu. You can't mess with perfection, right?"

Oma raised her eyebrows. She obviously had more questions, but she left them unspoken. Then she patted Alexis's hand. "No, the new owners were smart enough not to change anything there. Well, I'm going to turn in for the night. See you in the morning. Love you."

"I love you, too, Oma."

Alexis poured herself some coffee and settled into the comfy chair by the window. When she opened her laptop, a text message popped up. Justin. I'm sorry I had to leave. Please forgive me. Lunch tomorrow?

What did this mean? He wasn't horrified by what she'd told him? Or maybe he was, and he wanted to say it to her in person. Alexis wasn't sure what to think. Should she be embarrassed by what she said or annoyed with Justin for leaving so abruptly? Or maybe he really did have a work emergency? What kind of emergencies did realtors have? Her fingers hovered over the keyboard as she contemplated how to respond.

I'll be at Lake Haven tomorrow. You're welcome to come out and meet me there for lunch.

Alexis hit send. It was time to get to work. No matter what happened tomorrow, Alexis intended to have this video production plan finished and ready to hand off when she saw Justin.

CHAPTER NINE

Justin grabbed the bag of cheeseburgers and fries from the seat of his truck and got out, looking around for a clue to point him in the right direction. Mrs. Jacobson's Jeep was here, and so were several other vehicles. Work vans, trucks, and a backhoe filled the parking area in front of the lodge. The ladies hadn't wasted any time getting to work. The camp was a beehive of activity.

Finally, he spotted Clarice on the porch of one of the cabins speaking with Chuck Day, a local contractor. She waved at Justin when she saw him. "Hi, Justin. Alexis is down at the dock."

"Thanks, Clarice. Hey, Chuck. How's it going?"

Chuck gave a friendly nod. "Hey. Not bad. You brought lunch?" He hungrily eyed the bag of burgers Justin was holding.

Justin had enough food to share with Clarice and Alexis, but he hadn't anticipated providing lunch for a whole work crew. What now? He pretended not to hear Chuck's question as he hightailed it down the pathway toward the lake.

He found Alexis a few minutes later, walking along the shore as she spoke on her phone. While waiting for her to finish the call, Justin took off his shoes and socks and hung his feet over the edge of the dock. The cool water was refreshing.

"Hey, thanks for bringing lunch," Alexis said as she joined Justin, taking off her own shoes and socks. He noticed her toenails were a deep shade of royal blue.

"No problem. Again, I'm really sorry I had to bail last night."

Alexis shrugged, but her eyes narrowed. She opened her mouth as if she was about to say something but seemed to decide otherwise. Justin handed her a burger and a napkin from the bag, and they ate in silence for the next few minutes, watching the ducks bob their heads up and down as they searched for their own lunch.

"We're getting the dock replaced tomorrow. The new one floats. The company that's coming out to do the work, that's who I was on the phone with." Alexis swirled her foot through the water.

"I'm impressed with how quickly you and your grandma have been able to get everything going here. I can't wait to see what you do with this place. I hope we'll be able to highlight Lake Haven Retreat Center in the video we're putting together."

Alexis crinkled up her hamburger wrapper and tossed it in the paper bag. "Yeah. About that. I know we talked about filming that video together, but I know you're really busy. I think I can handle it on my own. I emailed you the production plan this morning. After you take a look at it, just let me know what you think."

Justin felt like a deflated balloon. Of course, she didn't need his help, but he was disappointed. He liked having an excuse to spend time with her. Now what? Had he done something wrong?

***

Alexis walked with Justin up the path toward the lodge to find Oma to give her the lunch Justin had brought for her. At this hour, she was probably getting hungry. It was anyone's guess if Oma would be at the lodge or not. She tended to flit from place to place around the camp like a little bird. Alexis wished she could call her, but cell phone service was spotty at best out here. Alexis had to go down to the dock to make most of her calls. She made a mental note to purchase some walkie-talkies so she and Oma could find each other when needed.

Telling Justin she could work on the project without his help had been her way of offering him a way out. She hadn't expected to see the disappointment on his face. Maybe she'd read the situation wrong? Would it be too nosy to ask about the call? She edged her way into the question she really wanted to ask. "So, that work emergency…is everything okay now?"

"Oh, yeah. A client of mine had an offer fall through last night. It's an amazing property, but he has nothing to worry about. I'm sure another offer will come through any day now."

Alexis felt the tension in her shoulders relax, but she quickly reminded herself that this wasn't all about her. Justin's words didn't match his slumped shoulders and the frown that pulled down the corners of his mouth. Of course, he was disappointed. She reached out and placed a hand on his arm. "I'm sorry the deal fell through."

"I have mixed feelings. I really want to buy the house for myself, but the timing isn't right." He paused. "I shouldn't admit this, but a part of me wanted the buyer to back out so I could have more time to get my finances together."

"Oh, yeah? What is it about the house that makes it so great?"

Justin smiled. "It's the cabin on the river that you drove me to the other day. Even though it's small, it has high vaulted ceilings that make it feel spacious, and it has beautiful handcrafted wood elements throughout the house. But it's the view that I love the most: those mountains."

"You sold me." Alexis grinned. Maybe this little hiccup is a sign. Maybe the house is meant to be yours?"

"I don't know. It would be a stretch, but anything is possible." Justin shrugged. "My first duty is to my client, though. I have to get him the best possible price, so if I try to buy it, that could present a conflict of interest. I'm sure he can get a better offer from someone else."

Alexis admired Justin's integrity. She regretted what she'd said earlier, down at the dock. "You know, if you're not too busy, it really would be better if we worked together on gathering the footage for the video. This whole thing was your idea. We'll have to wait a few months to get the outdoor Christmas shots, but we could start now by interviewing some local business owners."

"I'd like that. I'll assist you however you like, but you're the boss." Justin gave Alexis a friendly wink.

The slump of low energy Alexis had been fighting all morning was suddenly gone. She was ready to plow through her long to-do list.

PART TWO

CHAPTER TEN

Alexis stood on the lodge's porch and waved goodbye to the painters as they drove away for the last time. Four months ago, Oma and Alexis had set December sixth, St. Nicholas Day, as the target date for welcoming their first guests to Lake Haven Retreat Center. It had been an ambitious goal, and a few times, she'd wondered if they would make it. But now, with only two days to go, Alexis could breathe easier. Everything was coming into place. All of the cabins, as well as the main lodge, had undergone significant renovations. Gone were the dormitory-style cabins, and in their place were five private retreats, all worthy of the most discerning travelers. Each one had its own bathroom, wood-burning stove, and cozy beds fitted with luxurious down comforters and linen sheets. But, beyond those similarities, each one was unique. Oma designed three cabins with families in mind. The other two spaces were more appropriate for couples who wanted a romantic escape.

Alexis trudged through the deep snow toward what used to be cabin three. She needed to shovel the path again, but she wasn't about to complain—the snow was just what she'd been praying for. With the snow, she and Justin could finish recording their video for the contest. The unfinished landscaping was now hidden beneath a thick white blanket, making the camp appear to be a magical wonderland. As she stomped the snow off her boots outside the front door, she looked up and smiled at the small wood sign labeling the cabin as the Snowdrop House.

She discovered Oma in the main bedroom, fluffing pillows on the king-sized canopy bed that dominated the room. Her grandma was in her element and as happy as Alexis had ever seen her. When Oma noticed Alexis, she stood and gave a satisfied sigh. "I think we need to put a Christmas tree in each cabin. What do you think?"

"Hmm … it would be a nice touch." Alexis kept her tone noncommittal.

All five of the cabins were fully booked for the weekend. Oma's idea for Christmas trees in the cabins was a good one, and the guests un-doubtedly expected to come and enjoy all the traditional Christmas activities associated with a holiday at Icicle Creek. But did they have time to decorate trees with everything else they still needed to do? There was already a giant, lavishly decorated Christmas tree in the main lodge, which would serve as a self-service kitchen, dining area, library, game room, and common gathering place. Twinkly fairy lights and garlands adorned the windows and ceiling beams. The lodge was holiday perfection.

Oma folded a throw blanket and draped it over a chair near the woodstove. As if reading Alexis's thoughts, she said, "I have a friend I can call to do the Christmas trees. I'll check to see if she's available tomorrow. You've been working so hard, and I'm proud of what we've done together. You need to go have some fun."

Fun.

Justin was a fun guy to hang out with, but Alexis had put her personal life on the back burner the past few months, pouring everything she had into working on the renovations of Lake Haven Retreat Center with Oma. Now that Justin was coming out to Lake Haven tomorrow to help film some footage to include in the town's Christmas contest entry video, Alexis was surprised by how excited she was to show him around the camp and resume their work together.

Justin hadn't reached out to her a whole lot, either. Alexis supposed he was busy with his real-estate business. Sure, there had been some mild flirtation going on earlier, and she could acknowledge that there were some sparks when they were together, but the timing had been all wrong. Perhaps they were meant to remain friends only.

They paused their project while they waited for the Christmas season to arrive. The hardest part of putting together this contest entry would be deciding how to edit the video down to ten short minutes—the maximum time allowed—while still including as many of the features as possible that would be sure to impress the judges into naming Icicle Creek America's Favorite Christmastown.

Alexis shook her head, brought her thoughts back to the present, looked around the cabin, and smiled. She was proud of what she and Oma had accomplished. "We make a great team, Oma. I hope the guests will love this place as much as we do. Do you really think we're ready?

Oma flipped off the lights and moved toward the door. "As ready as we'll ever be. Now, are you ready to go home?"

***

Justin was at his desk, checking his emails a final time before leaving for the day. He opened a new one from Mr. Mangle. His client's home had been on the market for five months, with two offers that fell through. It wasn't at all how he'd expected it to go, as there was nothing wrong with the property. It was a gem. The problems he was having selling it were simply bad luck. These things happen sometimes, yet Justin wondered if there was anything he could have done differently. The message in the email was brief. His client had agreed to lower the price.

Maybe it was finally appropriate to revisit the idea of buying the Mangle property for himself. With a house in the country, Justin could finally get a dog. His apartment felt too empty at the end of a long day. Too bad his landlady would never allow it. It was time he got his own place.

Justin's long hours at the office were paying off financially, but it came with sacrifices to his personal life. He hadn't spent time with his friends or family lately, and it had been several weeks since he'd last seen Alexis. It wasn't as if they were in a relationship, but he'd been thinking more and more about how he'd like to change that. That sure as heck wasn't going to happen if they never saw each other. She'd been busy, too, but now, with the renovations at the camp done, maybe that would change.

Justin was excited to drive out to Lake Haven Retreat Center the next day to see what Alexis and her grandmother had done with the place. He glanced out the window—still snowing. Would he need to put chains on his tires? He would make it out there, no matter what, and he needed to be honest with her about his feelings. He needed a plan.

A brochure on Justin's desk showing two horses pulling a sleigh across a bucolic snow-covered landscape caught his attention. It reminded him that Alexis wanted to include footage of a couple riding the sleigh through town for the video—but now, he had a better idea. Locating the phone number listed on the brochure, Justin pulled out his phone.

"Hello, I'm interested in your sleigh rentals. Do you have any availability tomorrow?"

CHAPTER ELEVEN

The early morning sun was beginning to cast a rosy hue over the sky. As she entered the lodge, Alexis flipped on the lights and set her camera on a table. Justin would be coming at eight so they could begin their day of filming at Lake Haven and then around Icicle Creek. She wanted to make sure every detail was perfect.

Her eyes moved around the large room, taking in the twinkly lights of the Christmas tree near the staircase, the leather club chairs arranged by the stone fireplace, and the fourteen-foot-long teak table with benches that occupied the center of the space. She'd spent many hours rubbing oil into the wood, bringing it back to its original beauty.

Alexis stood still, enjoying the moment. After weeks of listening to the sound of hammers and saws, all was quiet. The camp was no longer a work site. The piles of construction garbage were gone, and she and Oma had cleared away all the dust. It was now a welcoming space where families and friends would gather and make beautiful memories.

Coffee was the first order of the day, and then she'd get a fire going. Alexis moved into the kitchen, off the main room. As she made the coffee, she listened for the sound of Justin's truck coming up the gravel drive. After they finished today's filming, they would be done working together. Would she still run into him around town? Or would they drift apart?

While pouring herself a cup of coffee, she began to hear what sounded like bells. At first, it was faint, but then they seemed to be getting louder. She walked back into the main room and opened the front door to see what was happening. A sleigh pulled by two white horses came toward the lodge. The driver waved and smiled at her. Alexis, though confused, waved back. When the sleigh reached her and she saw who the passenger was, her breath caught in her throat.

"I thought this would be more fun than taking the truck today," Justin said as he jumped out.

"I think it will work!" Alexis laughed.

Justin grinned, clearly pleased with her reaction. He came closer and gave Alexis a warm hug. She stayed close, appreciating his scent of soap and leather. His dark hair had grown longer since she'd seen him last, and it was now falling into his eyes. He'd traded his usual pressed trousers and white dress shirt with tie for jeans, a flannel shirt, and a down jacket. It was a good look on him.

Alexis felt her face grow warm as she realized she was staring. "Umm, would you like some coffee before we start? I just made a fresh pot."

"Sure, I'll take some. Thank you."

Justin followed Alexis into the lodge, giving an appreciative glance around the large room as he entered. Alexis called over her shoulder as she went into the kitchen. "Feel free to wander around."

When she returned with two steaming mugs of coffee, she handed one to Justin, who had made himself comfortable in a chair near the fireplace. He gestured toward the rest of the room. "I'm impressed with everything you've done here." He took a sip of his coffee. "You did a beautiful job. I'm just … blown away!"

Alexis could sense the sincerity in his words, and she soaked them in with pleasure. "Thank you. We have our first guests arriving on Friday, and I think we're ready!" She took a sip of coffee. "Today, I thought we could start by filming some video around the camp, but first, I need to get a fire going. You know, for ambiance … to set the stage and everything."

"Sure, let me help. I'll take care of the fire."

Alexis felt a twinge of awareness sharpen as a memory surfaced—July, the cabin in Colorado, Nick, the staged Christmas, the pretend relationship. All fake. And now, once again, she was staging a scene, creating an aesthetic, and using aspirational idealism to sell a dream. Love. Belonging. Family. Home. These were qualities she always strove to convey in her videos. Was she making the same mistakes all over again? But those aspirations felt closer now. More real. But was that wishful thinking? What if this, too, was fake?

Pushing those unwelcome thoughts aside, Alexis reached for her camera and began filming Justin as he arranged the kindling in a crisscross formation inside the fireplace. She had a job to do. This video entry needed to show the judges how special this place was, that Icicle Creek really was America's Favorite Christmastown.

***

Justin guessed that Alexis had hours of video footage by the end of the day, but she assured him this was the process and she'd get it cut down to ten minutes. They'd started the day at

Lake Haven—no longer a rustic summer camp but a picturesque retreat center with every imaginable comfort available to the few lucky guests who'd been quick enough to snag reservations before it was fully booked for the rest of the year.

Taking a sleigh ride into town had been one of the better ideas he'd ever had, especially since snow had fallen most of the day. He'd enjoyed every minute of sitting close to Alexis, snuggled under a wool blanket as their driver had taken them back to town on a trail through the forest. Alexis had an innate ability to notice beauty everywhere—little things that he often overlooked. Their video project helped him gain a greater appreciation for his community.

After arriving in Icicle Creek, fully decked out in all its Christmas glory, they'd stopped for soup and sandwiches at Mary's Diner before stopping to get some footage at the community skating pond, a Christmas tree farm, and the downtown shopping zone. Alexis was doing all the work, and Justin felt a little guilty for not contributing much more than an extra set of hands to carry her equipment, but she knew what she was doing, and he felt privileged to be along for the ride. Of course, calling what they were doing work was a bit of a stretch. Today was one of the most pleasurable days he'd enjoyed in a very long time.

Now, dusk was settling in, and more people began arriving on Main Street setting up chairs along the sidewalk as they got ready to watch the Christmas parade—a new addition to the town's holiday schedule of events. Several months ago, when Justin asked for help getting Icicle Creek named America's Favorite Christmastown at the council meeting, he'd done so with confidence, knowing the town's citizens would pull through. And they had. They'd gone above and beyond in their efforts to improve upon what was already a spectacular place to spend Christmas.

The sidewalk was getting crowded. Justin reached out and took Alexis's hand as they headed toward the park where various food carts were parked around the gazebo. After being outside all day, they were both starving. The aroma of sizzling burgers lured them toward the Waldo's Grill food truck. Alexis put her camera away and let out a contented sigh as they waited in line. "Today has been perfect. I'm excited to start editing this footage." She paused, then met his gaze. "You know, it has been a lot of fun hanging out with you." She took a deep breath, working up the courage she needed for what she said next. "I don't want it to end just because we're almost done with this project."

"I don't either." Here was the opening he'd been waiting for all day. "How about this: I take you on a date, for real—no work projects to distract us—just you and me, getting to know each other better." He waited to see her reaction.

Her lips moved upward into a smile. "Yes, I'd like that."

After Alexis ordered beef sliders and Justin got a bacon burger, they wandered over to a picnic table with their food tickets in hand and waited for their numbers to be called. A brass band was playing a rendition of "Winter Wonderland." Nearby, kids were running up a small hill with their sleds and barreling back down with shouts of pure joy.

Justin watched as a breeze pulled a lock of hair loose from Alexis's ponytail. He reached over and tucked it behind her ear as he picked up the conversation where they'd left off. "Would you like to have dinner and attend the Nutcracker performance next weekend? My niece, Amy, is performing."

"Oh, yes! I danced in the Nutcracker every year when I was a child."

"Okay, then. It's a date!"

Justin let out a deep breath. It was a relief to be open about his intentions—finally. He liked Alexis, and he was done hiding that fact.

CHAPTER TWELVE

After dinner in the park, Alexis scanned the sidewalk on the other side of the street, searching for an opening where she and Justin could stand to watch the parade. She spotted Oma sitting in a lawn chair next to her friend Lois. Lois saw Alexis first and motioned with her hand to come over. She looked at Justin. "Want to join them?"

Justin nodded in agreement, reaching out to take her hand as he led the way, dodging a group of elves headed toward the parade route's starting point. She loved the way her hand felt in his … warm and secure.

As they approached the two older women, Alexis caught the nudge Lois gave Oma, then the pointed assessment of them together, followed by raised eyebrows and shared smiles. Oma leaned over and spoke something to Lois, who nodded. Could they be any more obvious? Maybe bringing Justin over was a mistake, but it was too late to bail.

Alexis called out a greeting, "Lois, Oma … hello. Lois, this is my friend, Justin Karon. Have you met before?"

"I don't believe we have," Lois waved. "Nice to meet you, Justin. You two are welcome to watch the parade with us. There's plenty of room." She reached into a tote next to her chair. "I brought extra blankets. You can use this one to sit on." Lois handed Justin a large quilt.

Justin and Alexis settled in, grateful for the blanket and a spot to sit on the snow-covered curb—at least for the moment. There was work to do, and she'd be moving around as she recorded the parade. Alexis was readying her camera as the first entrants in the parade—a line of drummers—began their march down Main Street. After this, she would have all the footage she needed to put together a video high-lighting all the best Icicle Creek had to offer at Christmastime. She was glad Justin asked her to take on this project. It had been a gratifying diversion and a fun excuse to spend more time with him. Now—finally—Justin had asked her out on an actual date. Her spirits were flying high.

From the moment Justin had arrived on that beautiful sleigh, through dinner in the park, elec-tricity had buzzed between them. It felt like they'd been in a dream world, occupied by just them. As much as she loved Oma and Lois, their sudden presence among her and Justin was jar-ring, like suddenly being jolted awake. She hadn't been ready. Lifting her camera and push-ing record, she made herself busy.

An hour later, the parade was over, and Alex-is had finished filming. Not wanting her grand-mother to walk home alone, Alexis decided to join her, even though she would have preferred to spend more time alone with Justin. He said goodbye with friendly hugs for Alexis and Oma. It wasn't precisely how Alexis had anticipated the day ending, but at least she knew she'd see him again soon.

***

Alexis hit the upload button, leaned back in her chair, and rubbed her tired eyes. After being immersed in editing for the last few hours, she needed a moment to return to reality: Oma's en-closed porch in Icicle Creek. What time was it? Three o'clock in the afternoon? Already? This feeling of disorientation—after being caught up in exciting work and completely forgetting every-thing else around her—was something she'd missed. Helping Oma with the renovations at the retreat center had been satisfying, but telling stories through video was where she thrived. This video had been a labor of love. It was her way of giving back to Icicle Creek, a community that had helped her heal after her parents died.

Ten minutes. It had required some tough choices on what to keep and cut, but Alexis had done it. She'd taken hours of footage and edited it into ten fabulous minutes, showcasing the best the town had to offer. After Justin dropped her off last night, it was impossible to sleep, so instead, Alexis got up and began working. And now, the video contest entry for America's Favorite Christmastown was done. It was some of her best work. Alexis knew Icicle Creek stood a high chance of winning. The nationwide exposure would boost the businesses and be a sweet source of well-deserved pride for the citizens—if they won. They would have to wait until the week before Christmas to find out.

Stretching her arms overhead, Alexis eased the tension from her muscles. She let her gaze move to the window. Outside, Oma was filling a bird feeder. Now that their guests were happily settled in at Lake Haven, Oma was finally able to relax a little, too. Eventually, Alexis turned her attention back to her laptop and opened her YouTube account.

The promotional video she and Nick made for the resort back in July was finally posted. She'd scheduled it so long ago it had almost slipped her mind. Wow, it was really taking off! This was a surprise. After all those months without any new content, she hadn't had high expectations for its success. The resort would be happy if these numbers translated to extra bookings. She began reading the comments.

Nick and Alexis, we're so glad you're back! Where have you been?

It has been soooo long since you posted a video! What happened?

She scrolled along. There were hundreds of comments, with most repeating a variation of those sentiments. It made sense. She and Nick had disappeared from YouTube and their other social media channels without any explanation. Did they owe people one? Probably. Their loyal viewers had supported them over the years and made the lifestyle they'd enjoyed possible, but Alexis dreaded the idea of rehashing the ugly details of her private life in public. She'd probably have to record something with Nick. It had been nearly six months since she'd seen him.

Alexis typed an email to Nick, asking him what he wanted to do about the situation, and hit send before she could change her mind.

CHAPTER THIRTEEN

Justin parked his truck at Cascade Bank and went inside to meet Brett, his old high school buddy, who was now a mortgage officer. Mr. Mangle had accepted Justin's offer, contingent on financing, so he was here to secure a loan.

"Brett isn't in yet, but he should be here soon," the receptionist said, motioning toward a couch in the lobby. "You're welcome to sit over there if you want to wait. Can I get you some coffee?"

"Yes, that would be nice. Thank you."

Justin settled in, then checked his phone. There was a text from his sister, Elyse. Did you see this? It doesn't seem like she's single. Sorry. I just don't want to see you get your heart broken.

It was a link to the latest Nick and Alexis video. He didn't need to click on it since he'd already watched it. It was the one where Nick and Alexis were at the resort in Colorado, celebrating Christmas together, all cozy and romantic. His friend Matt had already sent it to him. Justin hadn't even gone on one actual date with Alexis. All the time they'd spent together had been under the pretext of filming the video. Why did people already assume they were an item? Or that he was some fool she was just playing with?

He knew the truth. That video had been recorded in July, right before Alexis moved back to Icicle Creek. It wasn't real—though not many people knew that.

He wasn't sure how to respond to his sister since, Alexis had told him her story in confidence. When Brett approached him, he was still thinking about how to reply to Elyse. Brett held out his hand, "Hey, Justin. How's it going? What can I do for you?"

Justin shoved his phone into his pocket and stood to greet Brett. "Hey—good to see you. Not bad. I found a house I'd like to buy and would like to talk to you about a loan."

"Sure, let's talk." Brett led Justin over to his desk.

Though the preapproval was already behind him, Justin knew the loan process was often full of bumps and sharp turns that could derail a buyer at any point along the way. It would be foolish to celebrate the purchase of this home until every last line on the paperwork was signed and finalized. Justin sat across Brett, feeling his heart race. Despite his best efforts to remain detached emotionally, he'd failed. Justin wanted this house more than he cared to admit. He slid some paperwork across the desk. "I can put 20 percent down."

A half-hour later, Justin left the bank. He'd filled out all the paperwork. Now, it was a matter of wait-and-see. His phone vibrated as he walked to his truck, but he ignored it. Needing some time to think, he decided to take a drive through the mountains.

Alexis's secret made him uncomfortable, but she had been honest with him, at least. He had his own secret and a sinking feeling that it could ruin everything if it got out—and he had to tell her soon. The longer he waited, the harder it would be.

***

Alexis watched from the lodge's front window as Maria walked from the camp's laundry cabin toward the recently vacated Snowdrop House with an armload of fresh towels and sheets. She gave Maria, the new housekeeper, a smile and a wave. Their new hire was proving to be both reliable and efficient. It was easier for Alexis to relax now, knowing that the responsibilities of running Lake Haven Retreat Center would not rest solely on the shoulders of only Oma and her.

Once they found a groundskeeper, their staff would finally be complete. She decided to work on a help-wanted ad for that position next; it could go in tomorrow's paper if it were submitted by three o'clock.

She'd made herself a makeshift office at Lake Haven by placing a desk and chair in the corner of the main lodge under two large windows where she could see the comings and goings of people at the camp. Opening her laptop, she checked her email first. There was already a response from Nick waiting for her.

> Hi Alexis,
>
> I agree. It does seem necessary that we get together and make one last video. We don't need to give too many details-- just explain that we're no longer a couple and tell them we won't be making videos together anymore. I would love to see you again. I've missed you, and I would like to see what you and your grandma have done with the vacation rentals you told me about. I have a few days off before Christmas. I can drive over from Seattle to see you. How about this Thursday?

Love, Nick

He'd missed her? Love? These statements were … unexpected. They hadn't parted on the best of terms. Whatever. He was probably just trying to be polite. Alexis typed off a quick reply saying Thursday was fine. Thursday was only two days from now. After another moment of thought, she wondered if she should have asked Nick how long he would be staying. She was going to the Nutcracker with Justin on Friday night. Hopefully, Nick would be long gone by then.

CHAPTER FOURTEEN

Alexis watched as Nick parked his Subaru Outback across the street from Oma's house. He was early. She set aside the book she'd been reading and rose from the couch. Drawing a deep breath, she mentally prepared to greet her former flame. She caught her reflection in the entryway mirror as she walked toward the front door. Her hair was piled into a messy bun, and her face was makeup free. A tube of lip gloss rested in a silver bowl on the hallway table. She grabbed it, quickly swiping it across her lips. Then, looking in the mirror, she rolled her eyes at the ridiculousness of what she'd just done. Nick wouldn't care how she looked. And why should she? Any feelings she once had for him were long gone.

She opened the door, and Nick immediately enveloped her in a bear hug.

"Hey, Nick. Thanks for coming. How was the drive?" Alexis's asked, her voice muffled against Nick's down jacket.

He let go, stood back, and smiled. "I got stuck behind a snow plow for twenty miles or so, but otherwise, not bad."

Yet he'd still arrived early? "Good, good ... well, come on in."

Alexis stepped aside, then noticed the bag slung over Nick's shoulder. Was he planning to stay overnight?

Oma, who'd been in the kitchen, joined them in the hallway. She greeted Nick with a warm hug. "Nick, dear, it's wonderful to see you. How have you been?"

With Nick and Oma engaged in conversation, Alexis took the opportunity to run upstairs and make herself more presentable—for the camera. The quicker they recorded this video and got it over with, the better.

After changing her clothes, running a brush through her hair, and applying some makeup, Alexis rejoined them in the living room. They were having coffee, and Oma had set out a plate of cookies. She caught the tail end of what Oma was saying to Nick as they stood together, admiring the tree. ".... Alexis made that ornament for me when she was in first grade."

Alexis knew her grandmother was unfailingly polite and would never be anything but welcoming to anyone who set foot in her home, but the cozy scene she'd walked into was a little too friendly. Something felt off. Oma glanced toward

Alexis long enough to receive the silent message. Oma cleared her throat. "Well, kids … I'll leave you to it. I know you have a vlog to record, and I've got a Bunco game at Lois's house I need to be at. See you later!"

After Oma left, Alexis began setting up her video equipment. She wasn't really in the mood for small talk. "Okay, what, exactly, are we going to say in this video?"

"Hmmm … well, have you had lunch yet? Let me take you out to eat, and we can talk details then."

Alexis didn't want to go to lunch with Nick. It was a small town, and someone might see them. She wanted to clear up any misconceptions people might have about the two of them, not make the waters even muddier than they already were. But Nick was probably hungry, and there wasn't much in the kitchen to eat. Why didn't she go to the grocery store earlier? Alexis tried another approach. "Or, we could order in."

"Nah, how about we go out, and then you can show me the property you and your grandma have been renovating."

She pasted a smile on her face. "All right, then."

Alexis resigned herself to doing things Nick's way today. Whatever it would take to be done with him and move on.

Half an hour later, they were seated across from each other in a booth at Der Pizza Haus. As usual, Alexis didn't need the menu. She already knew what she wanted— the Sicilian special—but she was using the menu to try and hide her face from Elyse, who'd just walked in. Elyse was a lovely person whom Alexis liked, and under different circumstances, Alexis would have been happy to see her. Just not today. Not when she was having lunch with Nick.

"Alexis, how are you?" Alexis lowered the menu to discover Elyse standing in front of her.

"Oh, Elyse! Hello … I'm good, thanks. Uhh, Elyse, this is Nick, a friend of mine from Seattle. Nick, I went to school with Elyse. She was a couple of years younger. Class of 2014, right?"

Elyse nodded and gave a little wave. "That's right. Nick, yes … I recognize you from the YouTube channel. Good to meet you."

Nick gave Elyse his most charming smile— the one he brought out whenever a fan recognized him in public. "Elyse, it's a pleasure to meet you. Yes, that's me; I'm the other half of the team." He laughed.

Why was Nick making it sound as if they were still together? Alexis felt her face grow warm. Elyse knew how much time she'd spent with her brother. News got around fast in this small town. That sleigh ride with Justin had set off an avalanche of speculation regarding their relationship status just before the video came out with her and Nick playing the part of the cozy romantic couple. Alexis knew that people had questions. Everyone loved Justin. She'd received many side-eyed glances from community members over the last few days. The unspoken message was loud and clear. If she hurt him, they'd have his back.

"Well, uh, I'm meeting a friend." Elyse gestured toward another table where a twenty-something blonde, who appeared to have come straight from a yoga class, sat watching Alexis with a not-so-friendly stare. "I'll leave you two to enjoy your lunch. See you around."

After Elyse left, Alexis let out a deep sigh. "She probably thinks I'm some kind of player, out to hurt her brother. They all do. Why did you make it sound like we're still together?"

Nick shrugged. "What do you mean? You … a player? Ha! What would make her think that?" He paused. "Who's her brother?"

"We put on a pretty good act in our videos, Nick. People are confused. They don't know we recorded that video months ago or that it wasn't real, even then."

"I'm not that good of an actor. Maybe some of it was real." Nick frowned. "And who's her brother?"

Alexis did her best to keep her voice quiet. She didn't want to betray how annoyed she was by Nick's question. "Her brother is Justin Karon. He's my grandmother's real estate agent and I helped him record a video for a contest. And what do you mean, some of it was real? You're the one who decided to leave!"

A waitress came to the table to take their order. Alexis took the opportunity to compose herself. Nick leaned across the table when their server left and put his hand over hers. She pulled her hand away. "Nick, I've moved on. I wish you all the best and hope you can do the same. We both know that we're better off as friends."

"I made a mistake, Alexis. I came here to ask you to forgive me. I think we should give our relationship another chance."

Alexis couldn't believe what she was hearing. Shaking her head no, she glanced toward the kitchen. When was their food going to arrive? "Stop. Please. Let's talk about this later. Not here."

After the waitress brought their pizza to the table, they ate silently. It was a long, awkward meal.

***

"Alexis, dear, will Nick be joining us for dinner tonight?" Oma called over her shoulder as she pulled a loaf of bread out of the oven.

"No, he went back to Seattle already." Alexis pulled out a stool and sat down at the kitchen counter.

Oma didn't hide the surprise from her face. "Oh? How did it go?"

"It didn't. He left without recording the video." Alexis sighed. "He wanted to get back together, and I told him I wasn't interested. Then he left."

"Oh, wow. I'm sorry, honey. Maybe he just needs some time to cool off. The holidays can be an emotional time for a lot of people."

"Well, he's left me in a lurch, once again. I should have known better."

Oma filled the teapot with water and put it on the stove. "Would you like some tea?"

Alexis nodded. "Yes, please."

"Now, tell me, why is it so important that you have Nick film this video with you?"

"I guess I just wanted some closure. I wanted to wrap up that part of my life—give people an explanation for why we disappeared from our channel." She paused before adding. "I want to spend time with Justin and not feel the disapproval from everyone in town because they think I'm some two-timing cheater who's out to break his heart!"

"Ah, I see." Oma reached out and squeezed Alexis's hand. "Sometimes, these kinds of matters are better solved with face-to-face conversations. Have you talked to Justin about all of this?"

"No, not yet—and you're right. I need to do that."

Oma nodded. "Do you really think everyone in town thinks poorly about you? Has anyone said anything to you?"

"No, but I can feel their judgment by how they look at me."

"Feelings aren't always based on the truth, especially when it comes to making assumptions about what other people are thinking. Sometimes the extra baggage we carry gets in the way of seeing a situation clearly."

Alexis considered Oma's words. "What do you mean by extra baggage?"

"Maybe it's time to forgive yourself. Let go of the shame you've been carrying over those YouTube videos you did with Nick. It's in the past."

"I see your point, Oma." Alexis moved closer to her grandmother, looping an arm around her shoulder. "How come you always know the right thing to say?"

CHAPTER FIFTEEN

The first act began. Alexis watched the ballroom scene unfold into the battle scene as tiny dancers in mouse costumes scampered onto the stage, waving swords. Justin sat up straighter as he paid closer attention, trying his best to distinguish his niece, Amy, from the rest. It was a tall order, as they all looked the same. "I think Amy's the one on the end, on the left side of the stage!" Justin whispered.

Alexis loved seeing this side of Justin: the proud uncle. It was sweet, and it only made him more attractive. She liked the fact that he was part of a close-knit family. The Karon clan had shown up in full force tonight to support one of their own. Some of them Alexis already knew; others, she'd never met. However, thinking about Justin's family brought Alexis's focus to the reality that it was almost time for intermission. She and Justin had come straight from Mandell's to the theater, finding their seats only after the house lights had already been lowered, missing out on any preshow chit-chat. However, Alexis had noticed his sister Elyse and their mother seated several rows in front of them;

there would be no way to avoid them. The closer the ballet moved toward intermission, the more the butterflies flitted about in Alexis's stomach.

Did Elyse know she was here with Justin? What would she think after seeing her at lunch with Nick? Alexis recalled Oma's words: "Sometimes, these kinds of matters are better solved with face-to-face conversations." The theater lobby hardly seemed the appropriate place to explain things to Elyse, but Alexis knew she might not have a choice.

When the curtain closed and the lights came on, Alexis took a deep breath and readied herself for whatever was to come. Justin turned toward her and smiled. "Come with me. I have some family I want to introduce you to."

Five minutes later, Alexis was in the lobby with Justin, pulling a smile onto her face as she greeted Justin's sister. "Your daughter was adorable up there. Is this her first year in the Nutcracker?"

"Thank you. Yes, it is. She loves ballet. Amy first saw the Nutcracker show two years ago, and she's thrilled to finally have her turn on stage."

Alexis appreciated how cordial Elyse was to her, but her tone held an unmistakable hint of coolness. Could she blame her? Elyse cared about her brother and didn't want to see him hurt. Alexis took a sip of champagne from the glass Justin handed to her. A moment later, his attention was pulled away when Gary, Elyse's husband, started asking questions about real estate. Alexis hoped her voice didn't betray her nervousness when she spoke. "Hey, Elyse, I was wondering if you'd like to meet for coffee tomorrow morning if you're available? I'd love the chance to get to know you better."

"Um, yeah … that would be good. Nine o'clock at Jack's Cafe?"

"Perfect."

A gong sounded, announcing the end of intermission. Alexis felt the knot in her chest loosen a little—just in time to enjoy the rest of the ballet.

After the show and some additional brief chit-chat with his family, Justin led Alexis through the crowded lobby and out onto the street. The moon was shining bright on new-fallen snow, and a hush had fallen over the town.

Alexis let her eyes rest on the scene in front of her. "It's beautiful, isn't it?"

Justin took her hand. "I love this time of year." He glanced down at Alexis's shoes. "It's still early. Do you want to go for a walk? Will those shoes hold up?"

High heels in the snow? "Uh, could we stop by Oma's first? I better grab some boots."

CHAPTER SIXTEEN

The crunch of snow underfoot was the only sound in the air as Alexis and Justin wandered along the path that wound through Riverfront Park. It was quiet for a Saturday night. Alexis was still wearing the clothes she'd worn to the ballet, only now she had her sturdy Sorrell boots on her feet. She could have gone to her room and changed her clothes while Justin waited downstairs, but instead, she'd opted for a quick footwear change in the front entry before Oma had even known they'd come and gone. Alexis had enjoyed meeting Justin's family at the ballet, who had been very kind and welcoming, but she'd had enough small talk for the evening. Alexis wanted Justin all to herself, and Oma—had she seen them—sweet as she was, would have invited them in for hot cocoa, cookies, and more small talk. But now they were alone. Finally.

Alexis led the way across a small walking bridge, then stopped when they reached the middle. Peering over the railing, she watched as chunks of ice floated down the river. Justin wrapped an arm around her. "Are you warm enough?"

She hadn't even noticed the cold. "Yes, now I am." Alexis rested her head against Justin's shoulder. "Hey, I've been meaning to ask. Did you ever make an offer on the house you told me about?"

"I did, and they accepted my offer! If all goes well with the loan, the house will be mine by Christmas."

"That's exciting news! If you need any help with packing, let me know."

"Thank you. I just might take you up on that. I should probably get started, but ..." Justin paused. "There's a part of me that won't let me get my hopes up quite yet."

"Why is that?"

"There's something I haven't told you yet, about my time in DC ... I worked for a Political Action Committee that ran into some legal trouble, and now my former boss is in prison for embezzlement and fraud. I didn't know what he was doing, but he used me in his scheme, which I felt terrible about when I found out. For a time, I was under suspicion, too. I was ultimately exonerated, but there are still some people who think I'm guilty, and my name was dragged through the mud. That's why I left DC and came back here. I know all that shouldn't have any bearing on whether or not I'm able to get a loan on this house, but I can't help but worry a little."

Alexis thought about her next words before she spoke. She sensed Justin's confession was a turning point in their relationship. He showed her he trusted her by sharing the most vulnerable parts of his life. She was glad she hadn't known this part of his past until she'd gotten to know him better. Hadn't she already misjudged him once? She trusted him now and knew he was a good guy. "Thank you for telling me. I'm sorry that happened to you."

Justin smiled and gave Alexis's shoulder a little squeeze. Then he pointed toward the downtown area in the distance. "How about a snack? I can smell the bratwurst from Tom's cart over there. Are you hungry?"

"Not really, but maybe if you want to share, I'll have just a bite."

After making their way back to Main Street, Justin bought a bratwurst covered in Swiss cheese and offered Alexis the first bite. As they wandered past shops already closed for the evening and admired the Christmas window displays, Alexis sensed they were being followed.

When she heard movement behind them, she glanced over her shoulder and discovered a cute, scruffy, yellow lab behind them. She stopped and held out her hand for him to sniff. "Where's your person, big guy?"

The dog licked her hand and wagged his tail. Justin laughed when it gave a little whine and sat down, staring longingly at the bratwurst. "Are you hungry?"

Justin offered the dog the rest of his snack. It was gone in one bite. "You've got a new friend now," Alexis said as she scratched the dog's head, looking for a collar. "He doesn't have any tags."

"I'm sure he has a home." To the dog, Justin commanded, "Go home, boy!"

Instead, the dog followed Justin and Alexis for another block before wandering down a side street. They were nearing the spot where Justin had parked his truck. "Well, it's getting late. I suppose I should probably take you home." Justin said.

Alexis detected a note of regret in his voice and took his hand. She didn't want to leave, either. "We'll see each other again in two days. We've got the America's Favorite Christmastown winner's reveal party to look forward to."

Justin pulled Alexis closer to him, then softly touched her lips with his fingers. Alexis ran her fingers through Justin's hair and brought her face closer to meet his lips, which were warm and soft. Sparks ignited as she leaned into his kiss.

When their lips finally parted, Justin spoke softly into her ear. "I've been wanting to do that for a long time."

The feeling was mutual.

CHAPTER SEVENTEEN

Sunday morning, Justin noticed the yellow lab as he pulled into the parking lot at Icicle Creek Grocery. The dog was hanging out by the front door as if his job was to greet customers. Did this dog have a home? Perhaps the owner was inside the store, shopping. Yet it was strange there still wasn't a collar. Justin patted the dog on the head as he headed inside, noting that its ribs were clearly visible. "Hey, buddy. How's it going?"

Pulling out his phone, Justin brought up his grocery list and decided what section of the store to go to first. His mother was hosting the big Christmas party the next day, and he'd offered to do the shopping. She'd invited the entire Chamber of Commerce and many other town contributors toward the effort to have Icicle Creek designated America's Favorite Christmastown.

Baking chocolate and flour were at the top of the list, so he headed toward the baking aisle. Walking by an end display of dog treats, Justin impulsively threw a rawhide bone into the cart for the yellow lab outside. It was the Christmas season, after all—a time to give.

After checking off every item on the list, the cart could barely contain everything. Justin's mom always threw the best parties, making it her mission to provide her guests with delicious food they'd be talking about long after they'd gone home. He was confident that tomorrow's party would be no exception.

Even if Icicle Creek didn't win the contest, Justin was grateful for the opportunity it had given him to get to know Alexis better. Just thinking about her and that kiss last night made him smile. He was proud of the video they'd submitted and was excited to give everyone at the party a chance to view it. He was sure people would love it.

Justin exited the store with his groceries and felt a stab of disappointment to discover that the dog was no longer by the entrance. As he continued to his truck, he heard a screech of tires, followed by a thud. Justin's heart lurched in his chest and he turned his head toward the road to see what had happened. As a black sedan sped away, the injured dog limped back toward the parking lot. Justin raced toward it as a crowd began to gather. "Does anyone know whose dog this is?" he yelled.

Carl, a clerk from the store, spoke up. "I think he's a stray. He showed up a few days ago and has been begging for food from all our customers."

The dog dragged himself nearer, then thumped down at Justin's feet. Their eyes met and Justin could see he was in pain. "I'm taking this dog to the vet. If anyone comes looking for him, here's my number."

After giving Carl a business card, Justin coaxed the dog toward his truck and gently lifted him into the back.

***

Alexis waved goodbye to Elyse, then relaxed back into her chair with a smile. Their meeting at the coffee shop had gone better than she'd expected. Alexis had made herself vulnerable, offering no excuses while telling the entire story of how she'd carried on the illusion of a false relationship with Nick for the sake of business. Then Alexis had confided to Elyse how much she cared for Justin. Elyse graciously responded with understanding and compassion. Now, Alexis felt as if she had a new friend—a real one.

Oma's advice was proving strong. These face-to-face conversations required more from Alexis—specifically, courage and humility—than the one-sided dialogue she'd initially planned to record on video with Nick. However, they were also more rewarding. The crazy thing was that she was now grateful that Nick had walked out on her and happy with how everything had worked out. Life was funny that way.

Doris, the owner of the coffee shop, came over with a carafe of coffee. "Would you like a refill on that, honey?"

Alexis glanced at her phone, checking the time. It was still early enough in the morning. "Sure, one more would be great. Thank you."

Doris poured another cup, then left the bill and a miniature candy cane on the table before stepping away to help another customer. Alexis's phone screen lit up, showing an incoming call from Justin. "Hey, Justin—"

"Alexis ... hey, I'm at the vet with that yellow lab who was following us around last night. He was hit by a car—and the driver just left!"

"Oh, no! Is it bad?"

"The doctor doesn't think any bones are broken, but he's going to do some x-rays to make sure, and they want to rule out any internal bleeding, but so far, it seems like he's going to be okay other than some soreness—and he's really hungry."

"So the dog was just wandering around by himself again? I wonder where he belongs."

"Yeah, he was hanging out at the grocery store. I'm going to put some signs up around town and get the word out, but I'm not sure this fellow has a home."

"So, you rescued him."

Alexis felt a fluttering in her stomach. Justin was the real deal. She'd already been falling for him, but now she knew, without a doubt, that her heart was all in.

"I guess I did. But I'm not sure what to do next. Can you come to the clinic and help me?"

"I'll be right there."

CHAPTER EIGHTEEN

Justin lugged a giant bag of kibble to his apartment as Alexis followed behind, leading the dog on a leash. The dog's tail was wagging like a metronome while he wriggled around in a mass of joy and excitement. It was hard to believe he'd been hit by a car only a few hours ago.

The vet had already cleared the animal for release when Alexis had arrived at the clinic. According to the doctor, there was nothing wrong with the dog that some good food, a warm place to sleep, and a little love wouldn't fix.

Unhooking the leash from the new collar the doctor had kindly donated, Alexis scratched the top of the dog's head. "I know someone will probably claim him, but what do we call this big guy in the meantime? He needs a name."

Justin shook his head, but Alexis noted he seemed to be holding back a smile. If he was trying to hide the fact that he was just as excited to bring this stray dog home as the animal was to be here, he wasn't very convincing. She'd seen Justin's eyes light up when the vet encouraged them to take the dog home until they could find a more permanent solution. He hadn't paused a beat before saying yes.

"I don't know," he replied. "Would that be confusing to the poor guy? But you're right ... we have to call him something." He paused. "How about Max?" Justin leaned close to the dog, directing the following question at him. "Do you like the name, Max?"

The dog licked Justin's face.

"I think he approves," Alexis laughed.

As Justin riffled through the cupboards in search of a bowl to put Max's food in, Alexis scanned the apartment. It was clean and minimally furnished. The only decor was some landscape photography on the walls. "Did you take these pictures? They're beautiful."

Justin set a bowl of water on the floor next to Max's food. "I dabble with photography a little in my spare time."

He watched Max slurp the water in great thirsty gulps and addressed the issue at hand. "I'm not sure what I'm going to do. I'm not supposed to have a dog in this apartment. But he probably won't be here for long anyway. Someone will claim him," he concluded with a sigh.

Just then, his phone rang. Alexis wandered out to the back deck, taking in the view of downtown Icicle Creek while Justin took his call. Max, who had already finished his dinner, followed her. Justin's apartment was cute, but it would be hard to keep Max a secret for long in a place this small.

A few minutes later, Justin joined Alex with a big smile on his face. "That was the bank. My loan has cleared, and the closing on my new house is set for December 24th!"

"Christmas Eve? Wow, that's great! Congratulations!" Alexis wrapped her arms around Justin and kissed him.

Justin kissed her back, then pulled away to meet her eyes. "Thank you for helping me today with Max. I think we need to celebrate. Can I make you dinner tonight?"

"Sure, sounds like fun. Are we celebrating your new dog or getting a new house?"

Justin smiled. "He's not my dog—yet. But he's welcome to stay if it comes to it."

"Do you want me to pick anything up at the grocery store? I need to go to Lake Haven and do a little work, but I'll come back later this evening."

"Oh, the groceries!" Justin slapped his hand to his head. "They're still in the truck! I'll need to run them by my mom's house" He paused and changed the subject. "How's it going out at Lake Haven?"

"Great! We've got solid bookings well into the new year, and we finally have a full staff in place. Oma isn't going to need my help for much longer. The business practically runs itself." As Alexis turned to leave, she glanced down at Max, then offered, "I can run the groceries over to your mom's house on my way out of town."

***

Max hadn't even been in the apartment for an hour before Ms. Thorn, the landlady, discovered Justin's secret. Justin was taking the dog on a walk, mulling over what Alexis had said to him right before she'd left. Was she leaving Icicle Creek now that Lake Haven was up and running? That idea was like a dark cloud covering the previously sunny outlook he'd had on his future.

Ms. Thorn stood in front of the entrance to the building and peered down her nose at Max. "I sure hope you're not planning on taking that creature into your apartment. As you know, pets aren't allowed."

"Ugh, well … he's not mine. I'm trying to find his owner. He was hit by a car today."

"Humph. That dog looks fine to me."

"Please, Ms. Thorn. Just for tonight. I'll find another place for him; I promise. He doesn't have anywhere else to go. He's a good dog."

Ms. Thorn shook her head and wagged her finger. "I really shouldn't allow this. Tonight. That's it. And if he damages anything, you're on the hook!"

"Okay, thank you. He won't be a problem."

Justin sighed after Ms. Thorn left and went into the building. What was he going to do now? He still had two weeks before he could move into his new house. Max would love it there. It offered a river to swim in, a cozy wood stove to sleep next to, and plenty of room to run. There was no way Justin was taking Max to the animal shelter where he'd be locked in a cage. The poor fellow had been through too much already. He'd ask Alexis tonight at dinner if Max could stay with her for a few days. She seemed to share his soft spot for the dog.

CHAPTER NINETEEN

Alexis greeted Justin's mother, Mayor Karon, with a hug in the front hallway. She smelled like gingerbread cookies. Her smile was warm and welcoming. There was something about the woman's mannerisms that reminded Alexis of her own mother. "Alexis, dear. Welcome! Make yourself at home. Here, let me take your coat for you."

Alexis shrugged out of her coat. "Thank you, Mayor Karon. Your home is lovely."

It was a beautiful home: spacious and, elegant, yet unpretentious.

"Please, call me Julie—and thank you. Your grandmother helped me decorate for the party. She's got the magic touch when it comes to those things. Oh, and I can't wait to get my eyes on what the two of you have done with Lake Haven! Justin tells me you've transformed it into a beautiful retreat."

"You're welcome to come out anytime. I'd love to show you around."

After a few more minutes of visiting with her host, Alexis followed Justin into the living room. Butterflies ricocheted inside her stomach. The big reveal was less than an hour from now. Would Icicle Creek win the title of America's Favorite Christmastown? Initially, making the video for the contest had been a fun diversion, but somewhere in the process, she'd really started to care. Whatever the outcome, Icicle Creek was Alexis's favorite town for Christmas. There was nowhere else she'd rather be than right here, right now. Being part of this community, having people in her life who really knew her, and enjoying the privilege of giving something of herself back to them ... this is what it felt like to have a home.

The party was well underway, with people standing in little groups, laughing, drinking champagne, and chatting amiably. The atmosphere was joyful and festive. In the living room corner, a woman played "White Christmas" on a grand piano. Justin selected a bacon-wrapped scallop from a table laden with delicious finger foods. "Here, try this. They're the best."

Alexis took a bite and closed her eyes with delight as the savory goodness touched her tongue. "Hmm ... yum."

Justin smiled. "Thank you. I made them."

Last night, Alexis had been thoroughly impressed with the spaghetti carbonara Justin made her for dinner—and now bacon-wrapped scallops. "I think I love you."

Did I actually say that out loud? Alexis clamped her mouth shut in horror, but her panic was short-lived. Justin leaned closer and kissed her lightly on the lips. "I love you, too."

Alexis felt her cheeks grow warm when she realized they had an audience. Oma was standing on the other side of the table from them, wearing a triumphant expression. Oma held up her glass in a salute and winked at them.

Justin took a glass and raised it toward Oma with a smile. "Mrs. Jacobson, thank you for allowing Max to stay at your house for a few days. I hope he won't be a problem."

Oma laughed lightly. "Not a problem at all. He's a good dog."

The piano music suddenly stopped, and they were interrupted by the sound of Justin's mother tapping a fork against the side of a champagne glass. "Hello, everyone. Thank you for coming tonight. It's almost time for the contest results to be announced. If you could please turn your attention to the screen in the library, you'll be able to watch the YouTube live stream event."

Alexis took Justin's hand and gave it a squeeze as they followed the crowd into the other room. A jovial man, who could easily pass as Santa Claus, served as host. He began by introducing the five towns that had made it to the finals. The room erupted in cheers when he called out Icicle Creek, and a picture of Main Street came onto the screen. Then they watched each town's video entry. Icicle Creek was the final one in the lineup. Though she'd seen the footage more times than she could count, seeing it again, this time, surrounded by friends, was extra special. She felt a warm glow of gratitude as she listened to their supportive comments and the applause that followed when it was over.

The Santa Claus announcer stopped his banter to give a dramatic pause, "And now, the town that has been declared America's Favorite Christmastown ... located in the heart of Washington state ...." He paused again. "Icicle Creek!"

***

Alexis plopped down on the couch next to Oma and opened her laptop. Oma looked up, smiled, then returned to the book she was reading. Max was sleeping near her feet, and the house was quiet except for the crackling wood in the fire-place. The next day was Christmas Eve.

After checking her emails one last time, Alexis planned to shut the laptop and spend the next few days disconnected from the online world. Over the past week, Icicle Creek had been thrust into the national spotlight. Good Morning America sent a camera crew to do a feature on the town. Even though it meant being awake at four in the morning to accommodate the East Coast time zone, hundreds of residents had shown up for the live taping at the gazebo down-town. Mayor Karon asked Alexis to serve as the liaison—not only for the morning show but for several other newspapers, magazines, and on-line publications as well. And then, there were the job offers. Suddenly, Alexis's videography and editing skills were in demand, but this time, they wanted her. Just her.

There was an email from Nick. Alexis let out a sigh before clicking it open. What now? She'd closed that chapter and had no interest in going back. Oma, who seemed to have an uncanny ability to read other people's thoughts, put down her book and waited. As Alexis scanned the words on the screen, she could feel Oma's eyes on her. I'm sorry. Please forgive me. You were right. I was out of line, and I wish you much happiness. If you still want to record that video, let me know. Nick's message was a pleasant surprise. Alexis shut her computer, then addressed her grandmother, "An email from Nick. He apologized!"

Oma nodded. "Good for him." She put another log on the fire. "Alexis, I hope you know how much I appreciate everything you've done to help me get Lake Haven up and running. You have been a godsend. I don't think I could have done it without you—but I don't want you to feel that you're stuck here. If you want to take one of those job offers that came this week, you've got my full support."

"Thank you, Oma. I don't know what I'm going to do. I'll figure it out after Christmas … but I haven't felt stuck. The last few months have been wonderful. I didn't realize how much I missed you, and Icicle Creek, until I came back." Alexis paused, "I like having you as a business partner."

"I feel the same way about you, kid."

Oma reached down and scratched Max's head. Max licked her hand, and she laughed. "And no one has come forward to claim this guy? I think it's meant to be. Max and Justin belong together."

"Yeah, Justin gets the keys to his cabin tomorrow. This will be Max's last night here with us." Alexis directed her next words to the dog. "We're going to miss you, big guy!"

Max wagged his tail in response. Oma raised an eyebrow as she directed her gaze at Alexis. "You and Justin. May I ask?"

Alexis laughed. Oma could be downright meddlesome, but she meant well. "Well, I'll admit I do have feelings for him, and we have a lot of fun together—but sorry, I don't have an answer to that question, either."

CHAPTER TWENTY

Justin drove his truck up the snow-covered driveway toward his cabin. After signing the papers at the title company, he'd picked up Alexis and Max on his way out of town. It would be Alexis's first time seeing the inside of the house, and he felt strangely nervous. Would she like it?

The cabin had sat empty the past couple of months, as Mr. and Mrs. Mangle had already moved south. Noticing the deep drifts of snow that covered the front porch, Justin made a mental note to buy a snow shovel. Alexis let Max out of the truck, then laughed as the dog bounded past them, excited to explore his new surroundings. There was plenty of space for him to run here. Max would be happy.

The wonder of it all didn't escape Justin's notice. He knew God had brought him here, blessing him with gifts far above and beyond what he'd imagined for himself. Last Christmas, he'd been fielding calls from reporters about his former boss and wanting nothing more than to leave DC for a simpler life in Icicle Creek. Now, here he was with a thriving real estate business, a new home, a dog, and Alexis. He'd never felt this way about anyone before. She was his dream girl.

Justin felt Alexis's arms wrap around his waist as he stood in front of the house. He looked into her sparkling blue eyes, pleased to see the expression of delight. "What do you think?"

"Justin, it's beautiful! I want to see what it looks like inside!"

They made their way up to the porch, and Justin put the key in the door. Alexis called out to Max, who came bounding over to them. Justin brushed the snow off the dog's fur before he tracked it into the house. "You're home, Max!" he announced as he opened the door.

The cabin seemed bigger now that it was un-furnished—a blank canvas. Sunlight poured through the skylight onto the light pinewood floors in the entry. Justin's eyes went straight toward the large picture window, which dominat-ed the entire first level. It opened onto a view of the river, which currently had large ice chunks floating downstream. He wouldn't have been able to take the smile off his face even if he tried. Today was a very good day. Alexis's excit-ed reactions as she moved through the space were everything he'd hoped for.

Alexis spun around, throwing her arms into the air. "This place is amazing. You did well. Congratulations!"

There was only one question left. Justin drew in a deep breath before he spoke. "Alexis, I love you, and I can't imagine my future without you. I don't want this to be just my home; I want it to be ours." He pulled the ring box from his coat pocket and opened it, offering it to her. "Will you marry me?"

Alexis's mouth dropped open in surprise. "Yes! I love you, too. Yes!"

"I guessed on your ring size. I hope it fits."

Justin slid the ring onto Alexis's finger It was a perfect fit. She wrapped her arms around his neck and kissed his lips—pure bliss.

***

Alexis and her grandmother had spent a leisurely Christmas morning together, opening their gifts and eating a breakfast of cinnamon rolls, fresh fruit, and hard-boiled eggs. Alexis was still wearing her pajamas at noon.

Oma had just won their game of Scrabble and was putting the pieces back into the box when she glanced at her watch. "I should probably get the turkey in the oven. What time are Justin and his mother coming over?"

"Not until four. And Max is coming too. I'll go get dressed, and then I'll make the chocolate mousse."

Alexis was having a hard time keeping her secret. She'd hidden her engagement ring in her coat pocket until she and Justin could tell their families the news together at Christmas dinner. Nevertheless, Oma had been watching her closely all morning as if she knew.

Thankfully, the afternoon went by in a happy blur as Alexis and Oma chopped, stirred, and sauteed delicious foods in the kitchen together. When the doorbell chimed at four o'clock, Alexis practically ran to greet their guests. "Merry Christmas!"

Justin's mother handed a casserole dish to Alexis and greeted her with a warm smile. "Merry Christmas! Twice-baked potatoes … thank you for hosting us." She looked around the room. "This is lovely. You know, this is the first Christmas that Justin and I are on our own. Elyse and her family are with her husband's parents this year. It was the quietest Christmas morning I can ever remember!"

Oma joined the group in the entry, reaching out to hug both Justin and his mother. "I'm so glad you both could join us. And Max, welcome back!"

Justin followed Alexis into the living room while Julie and Oma were still talking. He whispered into her ear. "I think my mother knows something is up. She's been acting funny all morning."

Alexis laughed. "I think Oma suspects something, too. I don't want to wait until dinner. Let's tell them now."

Justin nodded in agreement. When everyone finally gathered in the living room, he nervously cleared his throat. "Um, Alexis and I have some news. Last night, I asked her to marry me ... and she said yes!"

Alexis moved closer to Justin, her heart overflowing with happiness. Oma immediately started crying. "Tears of joy," she reassured everyone.

"Ahh, let me hug you." Justin's mother had teary eyes, too.

Max ran from person to person, wagging his tail, sensing the excitement in the room.

Alexis pulled the ring out of her pocket and put it on her finger. Both her grandmother and Julie made appreciative comments on how beautiful it was.

Oma settled into her chair by the fireplace with a contented sigh. "Tell us all about it. I want to hear the whole story."

Before Alexis began speaking, she paused to take in the scene in front of her: the Christmas tree, the candles, the fireplace, and Justin beside her. It was the perfect Christmas. And the best part was that it was all real.

Dawn Klinge is the author of The Historic Hotels collection. She enjoys writing both contemporary and historical romance novels that feature strong women.

Dawn lives in central Washington with her husband. When she's not writing, she loves to read, play golf, ski, or hike. Saturday mornings, she can often be found browsing through thrift shops with her sister. She loves eating good food but would prefer to leave the cooking to anyone else.

You can visit Dawn at her website, www.dawnklinge.com. You can also find her on Instagram and Facebook.

Made in the USA
Columbia, SC
29 October 2022

70194063R00083